CONNECTING WHO

ARTIFICIAL BEINGS

An unofficial non-fiction reference book based on the BBC television programme Doctor Who

Peter Grehan

CANDY JAR BOOKS · CARDIFF
2016

The right of Peter Grehan to be identified as the
Author of the Work has been asserted by him in accordance
with the Copyright, Designs and Patents Act 1988.

Copyright © Peter Grehan 2016

Edited by Will Rees, Shaun Russell,
Lauren Thomas & Sian Kinsey
Cover: Will Brooks

Published by
Candy Jar Books
Mackintosh House
136 Newport Road, Cardiff, CF24 1DJ
www.candyjarbooks.co.uk

A catalogue record of this book is available
from the British Library

ISBN: 978-0-9955595-0-9

All rights reserved.
No part of this publication may be reproduced, stored in a
retrieval system, or transmitted at any time or by any means,
electronic, mechanical, photocopying, recording or otherwise
without the prior permission of the copyright holder. This
book is sold subject to the condition that it shall not by way of
trade or otherwise be circulated without the publisher's prior
consent in any form of binding or cover other than that in
which it is published.

Printed and bound in Great Britain by
Marston Book Services Ltd, Oxfordshire

I'll start this dedication by thanking my wife, Jane, without whose indulgence, encouragement and support I may well have given up on my writing ambitions a long time ago.

It is also doubtful that this book would ever have been written without the existence of University of South Glamorgan's BSc (Hons) degree in Science and Science Fiction. I owe a big thank you therefore to Mark Brake and Martin Griffiths for designing and creating that marvellous course and for their subsequent friendship.

Finally I should mention the editor on this book, William Rees, whose contribution to making this book flow coherently and keeping me from departing on too many tangents was not inconsiderable.

INTRODUCTION

There are certain things that everyone associates with science fiction. Along with time travel, interstellar journeys, and aliens are artificial beings: robots, androids and cyborgs. In this book I'm going to look at robots and androids and cyborgs. All of them have some sort of artificial intelligence, something that the machines we build may also have one day. I will also look at the differences between them, where the idea for them came from and see how they've been used in *Doctor Who*.

As a young boy I was an avid reader of comics. These were the British comics of low quality paper and poor ink, but the stories more than made up for this. My regular weekly read was *Lion*, and one of my favourite characters in it was Robot Archie, who was always more than a match for any villain he encountered. He produced a very positive image of robots in my young mind.

My love of science fiction grew with me, and I would watch any science fiction on TV that wasn't on too late or considered to be unsuitable for my young age. Above all, I loved stories that had robots in them. I remember one episode of *Out of the Unknown* called 'The Prophet' that featured robots. This was in 1967 and the story was an adaptation of an Isaac Asimov's *Robot* series story called 'Reason'.

A year later I saw these very same robots again in *The Mind Robber*. The costumes had been reused by the production team to save money. This wasn't this episodes only connection to *Doctor Who* though; the theme music for that episode was called 'Ziwzih Ziwzih OO-OO-OO' and was written and produced by Delia Derbyshire in 1966. You may remember that she was the person who, together with Ron Grainer, created the groundbreaking *Doctor Who* theme. I was a ten-year-old boy when I saw the very first episode, but it wasn't robots that got me hooked. Rather, it was a collection of none-humanoid cyborgs called the Daleks. The idea of cyborgs was new to me, or so I thought. They'd actually been around for quite some time, and I hadn't realised that I'd already read about them in *The War of the Worlds* by HG Wells.

Doctor Who, however, was meant to teach us stuff! That's why the Doctor's very first human companions, Ian and Barbara, were teachers. Ian's subject was science while Barbara's was history. They were included to help explain the times and science of the places the Doctor was going to visit. One of the great things about *Doctor Who* is the way we begin to learn stuff without us actually realising it, and because it's fun to watch, we begin to develop a taste for learning. It stimulated an interest in me that, as I learned about science, history and science fiction, made all sorts of connections in my mind.

And that's the reason for this book. As the title suggests I will attempt to connect the dots in the Whoniverse and discover how the concept of Artificial Intelligence has informed the direction of the world's best sci-fi series.

In doing so I will also explore the impact other science fiction, mythological and historical tales have had on everybody's favourite Time Lord.

CHAPTER 1
Robots: Automata as Myths

In 1963, the same year that *Doctor Who* was first broadcast, *Jason and the Argonauts* was released. The story centred on the classical Greek hero Jason and his search for the fabled Golden Fleece. I was desperate to see this film because, for its time, it had some brilliant special effects that included fantastical creatures from Greek Mythology. These had been created by the legendary American visual effects master Ray Harryhausen. My two personal favourites from the film were the skeletal warriors that Jason and his companions had to fight, and the giant bronze statue of Talos that came to life and attacked Jason's ship, the Argo. There is something distinctly unsettling about an entity that looks human but obviously isn't.

This fear has a name: automatonophobia. It means that the sufferer fears figures that represent humans, including human-looking androids. The more obvious the human qualities of the figures, the more likely people are to be unsettled by them. While few of us have the full-blown phobia, it is quite common for most people to feel hesitation or unease when encountering these figures. It is something that horror and science fiction storytellers are able to exploit to create tension and perhaps also helps us come to terms with our own anxieties? Certainly, the writers of *Doctor Who* have made very good use of this staple of science fiction over the years.

The term 'automata' is a very general name for things that are constructed but seem to have a life of their own. These automata have a history that goes way back in time, well before the science fiction robot as we know it today appeared. Mechanical men are a lot older than you think! For example, in a piece of fantastical fiction entitled *The True History* (an ironic title by the way), a storyteller called Lucian of Samosata[1], who lived between 125 AD to around 180 AD, described his travels through the ancient Greek solar system. He was like an ancient version of the Doctor, visiting alien worlds populated by strange beings. One of the places he visited was a city called Lampton, where the inhabitants were the equivalents of the robots and androids of today's science fiction. Instead of mechanical men, however, these automata were lamps that had escaped from their human owners and 'lived' in a society that functioned in the same way as any typical city of ancient Greece, with homes, a marketplace and, very importantly, a class structure. Curiously, we see in this story an early example of the natural human inclination to mistrust any intelligent machine. Lucian and his companions are treated courteously by the inhabitants of Lampton, but they refuse the hospitality they are offered because they cannot escape the feeling of apprehension they get from these mechanical beings. Was this an early example of robophobia, or

---

[1] A city in southeast Turkey on the upper Euphrates River

Grimwade's Syndrome, as it was called in *The Robots of Death*? Perhaps this syndrome will replace automatonophobia as a term when robots become more common in the future?

This wasn't the only example of ancient mechanical beings. Throughout myth and history there are tales of people creating artificial humans, like the Asian poem the *Epic Gesar of Living*, in which a talented smith builds an array of animated holy men, officials and soldiers from gold, silver and copper respectively.

Automata don't have to be made of metal – what about statues, for example? In *Blink* we see the Weeping Angels, (which must be some of the creepiest monsters we've ever seen). Their impact comes from tapping into our cultural myths but with a neat twist: we turn them into stone. Unfortunately, it's only for as long as we are able to look at them; the Weeping Angels move when they aren't being watched, but when they *do* move, they change from angelic figures to something quite horrific, all teeth and claw-like hands.

The Angels were partly inspired by the children's game 'statues' (also known as Grandmother's Footsteps). Another inspiration came from an incident that occurred while Steven Moffat was on holiday. He found an old, fenced off church and cemetery with warning signs proclaiming 'Danger' and a weeping angel statue amongst the graves. Sometime later, he took his children to visit the location and found that the weeping angel statue had disappeared. Obviously, he concluded, the danger sign had been placed there to keep people away from the angel.

However, moving statues isn't a new idea. In ancient Greek mythology there is the story of the sculptor King of Cyprus named Pygmalion. He is said to have sculptured a statue of a beautiful woman from ivory, named Galatea, whom the Goddess Aphrodite brought to life to become his wife. Other legends spoke of statues that walked in Antium[2], while in Rhodes and Crete images were said to breathe and move their feet. So, is this a deep seated anxiety we have of objects that look so human we feel they should be able to move but never do while we're looking? Do you remember at the end of *Blink*? We see lots of flashes of ordinary everyday statues around the world. How do you know that none of these move when you're not watching?

To my mind *Blink* was somewhat influenced by the tradition of folk tales to be considered as science fiction. Like the Weeping Angels themselves the story pulls us back in time to when rational thought and the scientific method was rarely applied to a story of strange creatures and mysterious goings on. These were just accepted without any expectation to make them plausible. Today we live in a post Darwin and Einstein universe, and in a science fiction story if we have to make up some rules for how the universe works these should at least be consistent. *Blink* works well enough as a fantasy, but it and the other Weeping Angel stories seem sit more comfortably amongst those legends of ancient Greece and Rome.

---

[2] Modern day Anzio in Italy

The Keeper of Traken also features stone creatures. The peaceful Traken Union has a kind of automatic immunity to invading creatures. These Melkurs, as they are called, become calcified as soon as they arrive within the Union. The result is a litter of statues, each one representing a failed attempt to bring evil into an idyllic world. The Master subverts this defence, however, as his TARDIS' chameleon circuit transforms its outward appearance to that of a calcified Melkur. This gives him a safe base with which to execute his despicable plans on a society that, not having had to deal with evil for so many generations, is easy pickings. The Master's Melkur TARDIS is also able to walk around, though it still needs to remain unseen. For a society that contained no evil, the Trakens did seem to me to be incredibly paranoid, with heavily armed guards roaming the countryside, seeking strangers to accuse of being evil, and an administration that was only too happy to think the worst of them. Perhaps that's the problem with living in what you see as an ideal society. You become convinced that every stranger wants to take it away from you.

Statues are made of stone, so perhaps it's harder to imagine them moving. If you wanted to create automata that moved then you'd use a material that was more flexible, like clay, for example? According to the creation myth of Abrahamic religions[3], God created the first man, Adam, from the dust of the Earth. The Hebrew for dust is *adamah*, and some people believe that this is where the first created

---

[3] The monotheistic faiths of Middle Eastern origin with roots going back to Abraham

man's name came from. According to the Koran, God created man from clay. Greek, Chinese and Egyptian creation mythologies also describe man as being created from clay. Perhaps it's no surprise then that there is a legend of an automata made from the clay of the Earth, called a Golem. These originated in Jewish mythology and were said to be simplistic, unfinished men animated by ritual. The Chief Rabbi of Prague supposedly created the most famous Golem in the sixteenth century in order to protect the city's Jews. In one version of the story, the Golem had to be 'switched off' when it began to threaten the Jews themselves. Once again, we see the creation turning on its creators. It's a recurring theme when we're talking about robots.

Perhaps the best known example of the human artifice doing so is Mary Shelley's *Frankenstein; or, The Modern Prometheus*. Well known science fiction writer and critic Brian Aldiss suggests that it is the very first example of modern science fiction. In this story a human artifice, the 'monster', is constructed from the body parts of human corpses. The created 'monster' is both highly intelligent and rebellious towards his irresponsible creator Frankenstein. And once again we see this theme of the created turning on the creator.

There are two parts to Mary Shelley's title, however. The second part *The Modern Prometheus* links back to ancient Greek mythology. Prometheus, whose name comes from the Greek word for 'forethought', was one of the Titans. These were the primeval race of gods who were later defeated and usurped by the Olympian gods. In Greek mythology it was Prometheus, together with Athena, who was responsible for creating man from clay. He then defied the Olympian gods by stealing fire from them, giving it to humanity in order to enable their progress to civilization. Prometheus has come to represent the quest for scientific knowledge, but often this progress is associated with unfortunate consequences. Perhaps this is why he is linked to any lone genius seeking knowledge and whose quest might well end in tragedy. It could almost describe the Doctor's life, couldn't it? In Mary Shelley's book, then, there is the suggestion that Frankenstein, in creating life, overreached himself by mimicking God without truly understanding what he was doing. He was in fact a student, neither a Doctor nor a Professor, whose pursuit of 'unhallowed arts' led him to create the monster. Once he had done so he found he had no stomach for it. His reaction was to flee and hope that the creature by being left unattended would simply die.

Frankenstein is both horrified by what he has created and refuses to take any responsibility for it not even giving it a name. Never once does he make an attempt to help or educate the creature to whom he is, in effect, the only parent. Instead he abandons it, leaving it to finally escape into the world to fend for itself. It does a remarkably good job of it and when it later confronts Frankenstein it speaks in an articulated and knowledgeable way. It is while on a walk in the Alps that Frankenstein is surprised by the creature who has come to ask his creator to take responsibility for his actions. 'How can I move thee?' he asks. 'Will no entreaties cause thee to turn a favourable eye upon thy creature, who implores thy goodness and compassion.' This is not the ranting of some mindless monster, but a heartfelt plea of a soul in torment. He longs for an end to his isolated existence and to be included into Frankenstein's world even if only in a small way. It is this exclusion that has made the creature vengeful and bitter, 'Everywhere I see bliss, from which I alone am irrevocably excluded. I was benevolent and good; misery made me a fiend.' Science and its developments, even though well-intentioned, often have unforeseen consequences. Frankenstein made things worse by not being prepared to face those consequences and not thinking through his experiment in the first place. Far from bringing good to the world his work brought suffering and death.

In *The Rebel Flesh* and *The Almost People* a lot of these ideas reappear. The story takes place in the twenty-second century in an old castle monastery that has become an industrial facility. The workers there use a self-replicating fluid called the Flesh to create artificial copies of themselves. They then control these remotely to carry out dangerous, and sometimes lethal, tasks. In many ways, these copies or doppelgängers (they are called Gangers in the story) are like the Golems, albeit fashioned from a synthetic form of clay. They are mindless, incomplete humans that can only function through the directions of their human originals. Then, like the Frankenstein's monster of the movies, a powerful lightning strike makes the Ganger copies become self aware. They now have the intelligence and personalities of their human originals. They are, in fact, exact duplicates with all the same virtues and faults, and they are no longer prepared to be seen as anything less than human. Human science had developed the Flesh and Gangers to be expendable machines to simplify working with dangerous substances. It was a short-sighted approach that took no account of longer term possibilities or problems. The Doctor sums it up by saying, 'How can you be so blinkered? It's alive. So alive. You're piling your lives, your personalities directly into it.'

With the realisation that their Gangers have become self aware, the reaction of their human originals is much like that of Frankenstein's in Shelley's novel. They are horrified and frightened by their creations. Their first hope is that the Gangers will simply revert to Flesh, the equivalent of Frankenstein hoping the creature will simply die in his absence. As it transpires that the Gangers will continue to live, the human's leader, Cleaves, describes them as monsters; a mistake that should be destroyed. The Doctor's early attempt to build a dialogue between the humans and the Gangers is thwarted by an act of violence by Cleaves. This is a focused and intense act of rejection. They have the memories of their original, the everyday human memories of belonging, but now they have been excluded, shut out. When their creators refuse to consider them as equals, the created become vengeful and murderous in the same way that Frankenstein's creation does.

Like Mary Shelley's story, *The Rebel Flesh* and *The Almost People* examine what it is to be human. It is the despair and bitterness in Frankenstein's rejection that turns the creature from one capable of loving and caring into something full of bitterness and hate. What was worse for the Gangers was the fact that they weren't just perfect physical copies; they were duplicates with all the memories and personalities of the originals. It was a story that illustrated how human beings can focus on the differences between them while ignoring their similarities. This is a story that uses the robot as a means to look at the ability that human beings have of using relatively unimportant differences – race, religion, sexuality or location – to define people as the 'other'. Something not like us, to be feared, hated and, if possible, destroyed. Using the duplicate Gangers makes this a very good *Doctor Who* and science fiction story that is worthy of a close reading. It is in fact such a good example of robot stories that I'll be returning to it in a future chapter.

Perhaps because *Frankenstein* was such an important story in science fiction history, it appears in a number of *Doctor Who* stories. An early appearance was during an episode of *The Chase*, when the Daleks, in their own time machine, are chasing the TARDIS through time and space. In an attempt to evade their pursuers, the Doctor lands in a mysterious old house where they encounter both Dracula and Frankenstein's monster. The pursuing Daleks are attacked by these characters, and whilst they are distracted, the TARDIS escapes once more. The Doctor suggests that they had somehow entered a dimension of human nightmares where the fictional horrors of human imagination had come to life.

In actual fact, the location was nothing more than a futuristic theme attraction called the *Festival of Ghana*. Ironically, Dracula and Frankenstein's monster were both mechanical robots! I remember watching this episode as a child and loving it. To me it was like Hammer meets *Doctor Who*, and it showed just how easy it was to create new possibilities in the series. The revelation at the end, though, was something of a disappointment, for two reasons. Firstly, the Doctor had totally misunderstood the situation, and it shook my faith in his infallibility. Secondly, what had a *Festival of Ghana* to do with characters from British horror literature? Even at the age of thirteen, I had a vague idea that Ghana was an African country. My father, on the other hand, enjoyed the joke that the Doctor had over thought the problem and come to the totally wrong conclusion. That far outweighed the disappointments for me, because it meant I could share my love of the series with my Dad even if only for a moment.

Another *Doctor Who* story containing some Frankenstein themes was the very first Fourth Doctor (Tom Baker) story, *Robot*. It was an odd combination of elements from *Frankenstein*, *Beauty and the Beast* and *King Kong* (which itself had its roots in *Beauty and the Beast*). Once again, we see the construction of an artificial being: a robot called K1. Just like the Golem, its purpose was to serve mankind, and as with the Golem, it became harder to control. Like the monster in Frankenstein, it had not had the benefit of a childhood in which to process its emotions and become a relatively balanced being (something that most human beings have trouble achieving). This was further aggravated by the misuse of K1 for criminal and immoral purposes, including murder. Like Frankenstein's monster, it looked for a pure emotional connection with another being. It is the sympathetic Sarah Jane Smith who provides this, becoming the equivalent to Belle in *Beauty and the Beast* and Ann Darrow in *King Kong*. *Robot* is an atypical robot story because K1 seems to have emotional needs that make it more comparable to Mary Shelley's tale than most other robot stories.

It was an ambitious plot let down by budget inadequacies. I found the 'King Kong' section of the story almost embarrassing, with an obvious doll Sarah Jane Smith and bits of K1's body partially disappearing because of the use of colour-separation overlay. The most disappointing part of the story for me was that the Doctor had to use his car, Bessie, as a weapon delivery system for the metal-biodegradable virus used to finally defeat the giant K1. This seemed to confirm the total ineffectiveness of the UNIT troops. In hindsight it's easy to see that the story had originally been written for the Third Doctor (Jon Pertwee), who was after all the 'action man' Doctor, but it was disappointing nevertheless.

A more obvious Frankenstein related *Doctor Who* story was *The Brain of Morbius*. This was a homage to the numerous cinematic manifestations of Mary Shelley's novel. The stylistic elements in the story that mimicked those classics of horror included a dark forbidding castle surrounded by thunder and lightning, a character very similar to Igor called

Condo, and of course an obsessed scientist Mehendri Solon, building a creature from mismatched alien body parts. Even some of the scenes echoed the cinematic *Frankenstein's* iconic moments, like the encounter between a blind person and the creature, and the creature being hunted by a vengeful torch-bearing populace, in this case the Sisterhood of Karn.

In fact there are so many reminders of cinematic *Frankenstein* that it is easy to miss the significant differences in the story. This isn't just a just a mad scientist on an ego trip, wanting to build a living creature. Solon has a specific purpose in building a body. It was meant to house the brain of the criminal Time Lord Morbius. In essence he is a monster, a man responsible for the deaths of thousands, who has a body constructed that reflects his monstrous nature. There is no desire to join a social framework, just to conquer and avenge himself on those that thwarted his plans of empire and sentenced him to death. Morbius had turned evil long before he became Solon's creature. Unlike Shelley's story there is no tail of rejection leading to bitterness, but rather the reincarnation of an evil overlord. As with Frankenstein, though, there is arrogant and irresponsible science followed by unforeseen consequences, not least the arrival of the Doctor. The overreaching arrogance of Solon and Morbius leads to their inevitable downfall. Biological robots, especially in an age where cloning experiments have started to progress, are becoming a real possibility, and we shall see that they remain an important part of Science Fiction.

*

The Enlightenment, or Age of Reason, began in the late seventeenth and eighteenth centuries and was a cultural movement of intellectuals who proposed that society should be developed along the lines of reason and logic. The 'scientific method' was to be used to advance knowledge and challenge traditional established ideas based on religious faith. In a sense, this created a schism between science and the spiritual sides of human culture that still echoes today. I have noticed how often the theme of science and spiritualism in conflict crops up in places that you wouldn't expect them to. As an example, The Imperial Ice Stars from Russia produced a version of Cinderella on ice that would be worthy of an episode of *Doctor Who*. In it Cinderella's father is a clockmaker, a man of science and logic who sees the universe as a form of clockwork mechanism; a metaphor for the science of the Enlightenment. So when a gypsy fortune teller (the equivalent to the Fairy Godmother in the Disney version) arrives in town, he dismisses her and her crystal ball as just so much nonsense. However, the gypsy has a powerful influence on all the clocks in the town, one that the clockmaker and his assistants seem unable to correct. It is science versus mysticism. When Cinderella disappears after midnight has struck, she seems lost forever. It is only when the clockmaker and the gypsy work together that the error in time is corrected and Cinderella is recovered so that the story can have its usual happy ending.

Clockwork mechanisms can represent both science and technology and the Enlightenment's generally accepted model of how the universe works. *The Mind Robber* turns this idea on its head. The Doctor and his companions find themselves in the dimension of fiction. They are surrounded by events and creatures associated with fantasy and mythology that do not seem to follow any logical pattern. At the same time the Doctor and his companions are menaced by life-size clockwork toy soldiers. The function of these automata seem to be the same as those of any foot soldier in the series, to capture the Doctor and his companions, but the fact that these are modelled on toys make them all the more unsettling. The feelings of harmless play is reversed into threat and danger. That they are clockwork automata, where clockwork mechanisms represent predictability and consistency, heighten the estrangement we feel in this other dimension. The insidious advance of these automata is accompanied by the sound of a surreal clockwork mechanism, amplifying those feelings into one of dread.

Historically clockwork mechanisms became very sophisticated during the Enlightenment, and it was during this period that France was the centre for the construction of ingenious mechanical toys and automata. Jacques de Vaucanson (1708 – 1782) was said to be the most skilled engineer of all it was believed that he had a secret ambition to build an artificial man. Some of these automatons, like Wolfgang von Kempelen's chess playing Turk, went on to develop a fame and mythology of their own. These constructs led Descartes to conclude that man and other living creatures were themselves forms of automaton occupied by a spiritual mind. It's probably no coincidence, therefore, that *The Girl in the Fireplace* featured highly advanced clockwork automata and was partly set in eighteenth century France during the reign of King Louis XV. The robots wear Enlightenment-era clothing together with jester's masks, presumably as a disguise for their jaunts back to eighteenth century France, but it is these masks that are perhaps their most frightening aspect. This must be especially so for someone suffering from coulrophobia, an extreme or irrational fear of clowns. If Descartes believed that man and other living creatures were simple forms of automaton, it seems the clockwork robots in this story agreed with him because they had 'disassembled' the human crew of their spaceship in order to use the body parts as spares to repair the damage it had suffered. The robots in this story could almost be a metaphor for the Enlightenment. As clockwork automata they can be seen as a very futuristic product of the technology of that time, but they have no recognition of the spiritual mind that Descartes spoke of. The automata were products of pure logic and reason; there was no room for spiritualism, therefore they saw human beings as no more than other automata that could be a source of spare parts. Steven Moffat is known to favour fairy stories and there are perhaps many elements of a fairy story in this episode, but it is also a very subtle commentary on the values put forward by the thinking of the Enlightenment. Spiritualism is sacrificed for reason and logic to the detriment of our humanity. Were we to become creatures of pure logic and reason we would be no better than the robots in this story. What was lacking from the story, however, was an explanation as to why a spacecraft would need to be equipped with clockwork robots. Doing so might have added an interesting dimension to the story and placed it more firmly in the science fiction category.

We can see then that the image of the human artifice occurs in many cultures and time periods. Those robots we see in *Doctor Who* have roots that go way back into our history and are the latest manifestations of a recurring theme. The different automata we see in *Doctor Who* reflect the changes in the way we see the world. The Weeping Angels hark back to a time when the inexplicable was seen as some form of magic. With the beginnings of science we see an ambition to distil reason and logic into a purer form of being with possible disastrous consequences for what makes us human. Throughout there is the theme of mankind using science to mimic God and overreaching itself. What is created is often not a perfect servant but something that threatens to destroy us. They can be a metaphor for anything from nuclear weapons to climate change.

Next we shall take a closer look at supercomputers and how they are represented in *Doctor Who*.

CHAPTER 2
Machine Intelligence

When I was fifteen my father took me to see *2001: A Space Odyssey* (1968). The film was far more sophisticated then I had expected and unlike *Doctor Who* not a single alien made an appearance, though their existence seemed to permeate the whole film. One of my favourite characters in the film was the spacecraft Discovery One's computer HAL, an artificially intelligent computer and one of the most articulated and charismatic characters in the film. This was a deliberate statement by the director, Stanley Kubrick, on how modern technological man was becoming increasingly less social and articulate. Perhaps it should come as no surprise that HAL became the closest thing to a villain in the film.

We know that things that look very much like human beings can make us feel uncomfortable, but there is one unique characteristic of humans that, if exhibited by other creatures, is particularly frightening. I'm talking here of the ability that enables us to dominate the planet: *our higher intelligence*. Over the years, science fiction authors have written stories about rats, monkeys, apes and ants (amongst others) acquiring a level of intelligence at least equal to, if not greater than, our own and so being able to challenge us for world domination. Since the invention of the computer the idea of an intelligent machine has become one of the staples of science fiction.

There is a joke in the science fiction community: a group of scientists one day build a super-intelligent computer to answer the question, 'Is there a God?' When the computer is switched on, it answers, 'There is now.'

So, will the machines consider us dispensable one day? It is a question that Professor Kevin Warwick, Professor of Cybernetics at the University of Reading, answers with a resounding 'Yes!'. He paints a grim picture of a limited, subservient existence for man, whose role has been relegated to that of livestock or even just a zoo specimen. This reflects the anxiety of a lot of us when it comes to the creation of intelligent machines.

Perhaps there is an interesting parallel here with the Daleks and their persistent hatred of all other forms of life. They are brains with weak and feeble mutated bodies that can only survive inside a metal box known as a travel machine. The design of these travel machines is based on the life support travel machine used by Davros their 'creator'. Davros is a severely disabled individual whose solution to the mutated future of the Kaleds is inspired by his own existence. The Daleks are in effect a disabled species, each one of them existing inside the equivalent of a life support system combined with a mobility scooter. Part of their hatred must come from the jealousy they feel towards other 'healthy' species. They are technically adept, but have no creativity, nothing that can give them the joy of making something for its own sake and no appreciation of that which is beautiful.

To the Daleks it must seem quite normal to allow a computer to manage their wars for them. It would be able to analyse vast amounts of data and choose the appropriate and logical course of action to successfully conduct the war. The problem with this policy is that if they wage a war on an enemy possessing a computer of equivalent power that also uses logic, then each side's tactics become entirely predictable and can be easily countered. This was the premise for *Destiny of the Daleks*. The Daleks return to Skaro to find Davros in order that he can reprogram their war computer. This is necessary to overcome this very situation in their war against a race of androids called the Movellans. In the words of Davros, 'Two gigantic computerised battle fleets locked together in deep space, hundreds of galactic battle cruisers vying with each other for centuries, and not a shot fired? […] You have reached a logical impasse.' The Doctor also recognises the situation and is somewhat more upbeat when he tells the Movellans, 'You're caught in an impasse of logic. You've discovered the recipe for everlasting peace. Congratulations. I'm terribly pleased.' This is, of course, not what the Movellans want to hear.

It seems to be an assumption that people will leave their most terrible weapons in the control of computers. I suppose this has the advantage of allowing you to start a war and leave the computer in charge of the dirty work. When I was a child, I read a Captain Condor story in the *Lion* comic. It was called *The Push Button Planet* and it depicted a totally automated war between two continents on the planet Algol IV. Two rival supercomputers each run the war efforts of their respective sides, launching attacks and counter-attacks by sending robot aircraft, ships and troops to probe the defences of the enemy computer's territory and then dispatching recovery units to repair damage to their own infrastructure. Any salvaged robots that can't be repaired are recycled, together with the wreckage of enemy robots, and melted down in the furnaces in readiness for the production of new robots.

Non-machines are ignored in this war. People and animals are regarded as irrelevant by the robot combatants, although the populace has been forced to move underground to avoid being killed in the crossfire. The supercomputers just do the job they were constructed for, and they do it very efficiently. There is no hate or malice in their make-up; they simply perform their assigned role.

In this way they are similar to Mentalis in *The Armageddon Factor*. Mentalis was built to conduct the war against Atrios. It did so in a logical way, without hatred, fear or guilt. This was in contrast to the commander of the Atrios forces, the Marshal of Atrios, who was a man full of ambition, deceit and arrogance. The Atrios would seem to come out favourably in a comparison between the two, yet the Marshall failed to get any of his attacks delivered while the Mentalis succeeded in killing millions. The idea that a super-intelligent computer on a depopulated planet could wage war against a society was an interesting one, much more interesting than the *Key to Time* story arch that reached its conclusion in this adventure.

Mentalis, though, was one of the successes of *The Armageddon Factor*, especially as communications had to be conducted via K9, preventing any human-like characteristics being exhibited by the machine while allowing K9 to work to his strengths. The story also illustrates the contrast between a machine's emotionless intelligence and human intelligence driven by emotion.

Might intelligent computers go insane? If we look at the different superintelligent computers that have appeared in *Doctor Who*, it's hard not to feel that they've all gone a little bonkers. One story where there is no doubt about this is *The Face of Evil*. The computer in question is called Xoanon and is suffering from a multiple personality disorder, the result of a previous intervention from the Doctor when he forgot to wipe his personality print from the computer's core after repairing it. Xoanon sounds a little like Hosanna, the shout of praise for Christ from the New Testament. This immediately gives us a clue as to which direction this story will take. The story's premise is a primitive tribe dealing with the advanced technology of an intelligent computer. It is a situation that science fiction author Arthur C Clarke described as a 'sufficiently advanced technology being indistinguishable from magic.' In this case the difference between the technologies has created a whole set of religious beliefs and two divergent cultures. The idea of a crew of a starship regressing into primitive and separate tribal societies following some disaster echoes the plot of Brian Aldiss' novel *Non-Stop* (1958). The events take place on-board a vast generational star ship which has become overrun with a jungle like vegetation. It is a very strange alien world of jungle mixed together with metal alloy corridors and chambers. These are two great anthropological stories, but that's something for a different *Connecting Who* book!

In *The Face of Evil* there are invisible phantoms that the Doctor suggests are 'Projections from the dark side of Xoanon's id.' This was an idea borrowed from a film called *Forbidden Planet* (1956) in which a very advanced alien race known as the Krell built a super machine that they used to amplify and then convert their thoughts into energy servitors. These were rather like invisible robot servants made of pure energy that had almost limitless power. Unfortunately for the Krell, the machine amplified thoughts from all the levels of their mind, including those from the id.

The founding father of psychoanalysis Sigmund Freud described the id as being filled with 'a striving to bring about the satisfaction of the instinctual needs.' Normally it would be controlled by the ego and super-ego of the mind, but the machine responded to all the very basic and selfish id's demands in the same way as any other parts of the mind, with disastrous consequences for the Krell. As one of the characters in the film puts it: 'the Krell forgot one thing... [the] monsters from the id!' The fact that Xoanon had an id suggests that super intelligent computers are structured very much on our own minds, with all the potential for mental disorders that we have, but with far more ability to wreak havoc on us. Obviously, the Krell machine that amplified thoughts had little or no intelligence to differentiate between the destructive thoughts of the id and conscious thoughts. Perhaps the Krell didn't trust supercomputers either?

I remember as a child seeing a TV clip of the invisible monster from the id of Dr Edward Morbius attacking the crew of United Planets Cruiser C57-D. It literally did look like some sort of demon as its towering shape became visible within the ship's force field and the fire from the crew's energy weapons. There was another clip featuring Robby the Robot, who had been built by Dr Morbius. This was no actor in a tin suit, but a sophisticated ground breaking film robot design. I was in my formative years and I wanted more, so at around the same time the following Saturday, I informed my father that I couldn't stay to 'help' him wash the car because I had to go in and watch some more about the robot and invisible monsters. I was disappointed to learn that this wasn't how a TV film-review programme worked. Obviously I was ready for the weekly episode format of *Doctor Who*, something to get me looking forward to a particular time on a Saturday afternoon.

It seems very possible that *2001: A Space Odyssey* influenced the writers of *The Face of Evil*. Xoanon had initially started life as the ship's computer for an expedition of human colonists known as the Mordee. The ship had crash landed and the computer had been damaged. The botched repair by the Doctor then caused it to have mental health problems. This reflected the role of HAL in 2001 since that part of the story concerns the mental breakdown of HAL. As the ship's computer, HAL had enormous responsibility for the success of the mission to the moons of Jupiter. What tipped it over the edge of sanity, though, was the pressure of being made to lie. The command to do something very, and possibly uniquely, human created an irresolvable conflict in the mind of HAL, and this caused him to have a mental breakdown and commit murder.

On board a spacecraft in the cold and dark vacuum of space, human beings are very much at the mercy of a ship's computer that has control of their life support systems. But what about those computers that threaten us on terra firma? Of course a brain in a box can't do a great deal unless it can control all the nuclear warheads on the planet. It needs hands and limbs to do its bidding. In science fiction intelligent machines seem to get around this problem.

In *The Mind Robber* events take place in an alternate fictional universe, where subordinate robots and clockwork toy soldiers reign free. In the 'real' world, however, things are slightly more practical. For example, in *The War Machines*, a supercomputer with Artificial Intelligence called WOTAN (Will Operating Thought ANalogue) takes control of human minds in order to create a slave workforce for itself. The enslaved are forced to build WOTAN an army of subordinate robot fighting machines. The Doctor needs to defeat WOTAN before it can link up with a worldwide computer network and become unstoppable. Those scenes in the warehouse still make me smile today, with its stacks of obviously empty cardboard boxes being scattered by an activated war machine. Although it received a great deal of criticism at the time, this was a very forward-looking story, pre-dating *Terminator 3: Rise of the Machines* (2003) by many decades and hinting at a Skynet-like outcome should WOTAN succeed in linking up with other world computers. The war machines themselves even looked a little like the slow(ish), cumbersome first wave robots from *Rise of the Machines*. This was also a story that hinted at the UNIT format that would dominate Jon Pertwee's Third Doctor era, with the character of the Doctor becoming almost an establishment figure.

It seems that the idea that static AI computers can create brainwashed human slaves is such a convenient one for the writers. It reappeared again in *The Green Death* in which a megalomaniacal AI supercomputer called BOSS (Bimorphic Organisational Systems Supervisor) creates a workforce of brainwashed humans. The name BOSS gives us a clue as to who is the mastermind behind this evil scheme. While the idea of a supercomputer brainwashing humans to do its bidding, as well as its plan to link up with other world computers, is without question the same as that of *The War Machines*, there are some important differences.

Firstly, *The Green Death* was an environmental story, the tale of an oil company versus environmentalists – something that still has relevance today. Another difference was that BOSS envied human creativity. BOSS tackled this desire by analysing and then reprogramming itself to acquire it. As BOSS explained to the Doctor, '[The] secret of human creativity is inefficiency. The human brain is a very poor computer indeed. It makes illogical guesses which turn out to be more logical than logic itself.' That's quite a compliment from a supercomputer. The process of BOSS acquiring creativity was also quite creative in itself. Without having creativity to start with, would it have been able to acquire it? When the Doctor challenges BOSS's claim of infallibility by presenting him with a conundrum – 'If I were to tell you that the next thing I say will be true but that the last thing I said was a lie, would you believe me?' – BOSS attempts to wheedle out of the question by claiming that, 'Er, the matter is not relevant.' At the same time it feels compelled to try and solve the insolvable. It is driven by an exaggerated sense of self-importance, and although it knows the statement is illogical, it finds it impossible to let it go. It seems that with human creativity comes human emotions, and BOSS seems to have acquired some of the bad ones.

From watching *Doctor Who* and other science fiction, it would be easy to think that supercomputers are a bad idea. Usually, they are only significant characters in stories when they go wrong. Sometimes, though, supercomputers can turn out to be a wonderful benefit. An example of this is CAL, the computer in *Silence in the Library* and *Forest of the Dead*. The events take place on an unnamed planet in the fifty-first century that is simply referred to as 'The Library'. Its entire surface has been used to create a library that houses the collected works of humankind. The library is constructed by a presumably fabulously wealthy man named Lux. It seems bizarre that a library in the fifty-first century would actually house a collection of paper books, and it would certainly take an entire planet to house the complete works of humankind in the fifty-first century. What is so strange, in this age of the e-book, is that the library wasn't an e-collection housed inside the giant computer that was there any way! This is even more perplexing when we are told that the computer is constructed at the core of the library to allow Lux's terminally ill daughter's mind to live on among the collected works of humankind. Surely a collection of e-books would therefore have been better so that his daughter's 'mind' could actually read them? The giant computer's name, CAL, is an acronym of Charlotte's initials: Charlotte Abigail Lux. The fact that there was a young girl's mind housed in the computer certainly made it a compassionate and caring machine, because CAL devises a means of saving thousands of people's lives by teleporting them into the matrix of the computer. They would otherwise have fallen victim to the piranha-like Vashta Nerada. CAL also allows them to live fulfilling virtual lives within its systems, despite putting itself under enormous strain in doing so.

Lux is an interesting choice of name; it comes from the Greek for light and is used as the SI[1] unit for light measurement. The Vashta Nerada are creatures of the dark forests, preferring and mimicking shadows. Light is their enemy and is represented by CAL. This was also one of two stories written by Steven Moffat that referenced the destruction of forests (the other being *The Doctor, the Widow and the Wardrobe*).

---

[1] International System of Units (abbreviated SI from French: *Le Système international d'unités*)

Forests seem to be a theme that he likes to return to. This is probably because of an association in many cultures between forests and fairy stories and myths. To the civilized mind, forests are the abode of strange and mysterious creatures. The Vashta Nerada's home was logged to destruction to create the books in the Library, and it is because of this that they lay claim to Library. There is a theme of 'nature biting back' to the story. If forests represent the mystical and spiritual, then their exploitation by corporate science and technology can be seen as a blinkered and arrogant perception of the universe. Knowing the process of photosynthesis and assigning names to the structure of a tree might be knowledge, but it is not true understanding. It takes us back to the Enlightenment and the schism between science and spiritualism. Above all it reminds us of hubris of knowledge and the perils of playing god as represented by Frankenstein.

A population living within a computer system is not a new idea. Most famously, this was the premise of *The Matrix* trilogy. The main character, Neo, wakes from his reality to find that he was one of billions of people maintained within individual pods as a source of bioelectrical energy for intelligent machines. He later learns that these machines were originally the invention of humankind and that there has been a war between the creators and their creations. In this war the humans had attempted to defeat the machines by blocking out sunlight and starving the machines of the solar energy by which they were powered. In response, the machines then created bioelectrical pods in order to allow them to use humans as an alternative power source. The humans trapped in this way experience a simulated world created by the machines.

A less sinister version of this idea occurs in the science fiction novel *Permutation City* by Greg Egan. The novel explores the nature of humanity and at what hypothetical point we stop being human. A number of people in the novel have their brains scanned so that their 'brain emulations' can be downloaded onto a vast cloud computer. In effect, their consciousness, or rather a copy of their consciousness, has been downloaded into a computer simulation where it can exist independently of their physical selves. Very rich people have begun to duplicate themselves in this way as a form of survival insurance for their minds. Once within the computer system, people begin to experiment with their physical forms, losing touch with what defines them physically as human.

The important difference between this and the people downloaded in *Silence in the Library* and *Forest of the Dead* is that the latter were physically uploaded in order to keep their bodies safe (to prevent the Vashta Nerada from eating them). CAL did this by utilizing a teleport system and storing the population's physical energy pattern inside a storage buffer. In effect, they were downloaded both physically and mentally. This in itself wasn't a new idea. It was used in a *Star Trek: The Next Generation* story 'Relics', in which former Starfleet officer Captain Montgomery Scott (better known as Scotty) sustains his 'life signal' in a transporter pattern buffer as a means of survival following the crash of the starship he was travelling in. Unlike the two *Doctor Who* episodes, however, his consciousness was not able to exist in any virtual world. He was recovered and restored as a physical being seventy-five years later, but from his point of view it was as if no time had passed at all.

The premise of *Star Trek* is that of a utopian existence, an age of plenty, made possible by well understood and compliant technologies. The human need for struggle and striving is catered for through the exploration of space and the challenges that are encountered in doing so. That is not to say that villainous computers and deadly robots haven't been encountered, but these are the problems of isolated communities outside the influence of the Federation of Planets and requiring the intervention of Star Fleet to solve the problems created.

For a series like *Doctor Who* that travels backward and forward in time it is more a case of stumbling across problems that have often occurred because of the predatory nature of one alien species or another. But the overriding theme with regard to humanity and technology is the need for caution. Humans are depicted as rushing headlong into technological developments either for corporate financial gain or personnel gratification and glorification. Technologies are developed without understanding their true potential and ramifications or how they will react given totally unforeseen circumstances. We are an infant species playing with the fire stolen from the gods for us by Prometheus. This applies as much to artificial intelligence as it does to genetically modified food, fracking and nuclear power.

Occasionally, intelligent computers in *Doctor Who* and other science fiction serve no real purpose in the plot other than being a source of useful information. This saves time and enables a plot to move along without all that tedious working things out or obvious info dumps. An example of this occurs in *The Girl Who Waited*, in which there is a computer complex where the patients (in this case Amy Pond) interact via the Interface. The Interface appears early on and describes itself as 'your guide, your teacher, your friend.' Immediately, it is established as a source of information, something for Amy to look to for reference. When Amy seeks a safe hiding place from the Handbots, it is the Interface that provides her with the information. In this way, complications in the plot are avoided, allowing a low budget episode to flow to its strengths. The Doctor can just about get away with knowing lots of stuff and working out how to solve problems on the run, but a girl from the twenty-first century needs help for us to believe she can survive in an alien world. For the same reason a series like *Red Dwarf* has a seemingly all-knowing android called Kryten and an occasionally useful supercomputer with dementia called Holly to provide the otherwise ignorant crew with the technical information they need to progress the story along smoothly.

What *Doctor Who* reminds us is that when it comes to the artificially intelligent computer we are like Frankenstein, embarking on creating life within the machine. If we ever succeed we had better be prepared to face up to the consequences and maybe show compassion to whatever it is we create. Perhaps reconnecting with the humility of our spiritual sides may prevent the sort of hubris that created much pain and grief for Frankenstein. From a story telling point of view the problem with static computers is that there is only so much you can do with them to create an interesting narrative, and in almost every case they need something else to extend the reach of their power that will create and maintain our interest. Robots and androids, though, are different. With them, as we shall see, the possibilities seem endless.

CHAPTER 3
The Biological Robot

One of my early experiences of TV science fiction was during 1963. It was the puppet series *Space Patrol*, and I especially enjoyed the robots that it featured. The robots were an essential part of what was depicted as a utopian existence. They were a tireless labour force that could work in the most hazardous of conditions. Above all, they were required to supervise the featured spacecraft, Galasphere 347 (aka Galasphere 024), while the Human, Martian and Venusian crewmembers were in suspended animation during their long voyages to the planets of the Solar System. It was unusual, especially for a children's puppet series, to accurately reflect the real vast distances involved.

One of the most exciting episodes for me was called 'The Robot Revolution'. An undersea volcanic eruption triggers a malfunction in the robots, causing them to go on the rampage and attempt to take over the world. It is that recurring theme again: the created turning on their creators. This series predated *Doctor Who* by only seven months, but it pipped it to the post for having the first entirely electronic TV theme. Even today, the combination of planetary images and eerie, out of this world music stands up well.

At that age I assumed that robots would be

manufactured in a similar way to cars or washing machines: on a production line with components bashed out of metal or moulded in plastic being added as it travelled along. I discovered later that robots and androids aren't always made of metal and plastic. Sometimes they can be made from living substances.

There is a race of *Doctor Who* who, although not actually built by another species, demonstrate the idea of a biological robot. These are the Ood, and we see them for the first time in *The Impossible Planet*. They are described by the humans in this episode as not only 'wanting' to serve, but actually requiring orders to be able to survive. It is as though they had evolved to be biological robots themselves, although the Doctor subsequently voices his belief that no species could naturally evolve to be servants. Of course, it transpires that the Ood are not born to serve at all; instead they had been enslaved and actively converted into obedient biological robots. The Ood are first seen carrying translation spheres that are connected to their brains. These enabled them, as a telepathic species, to communicate to non-telepathic humans. We learn in *The Planet of the Ood* that the translation spheres actually replace an external brain, a 'hindbrain', in which the individual Ood's personality is contained. Removing this make the Ood suitable for service to humans, a process that Donna Noble, the Doctor's companion, describes as lobotomising them. As a telepathic species the Ood also share a collective consciousness through their living Hive mind. Ood Operations, the human run corporation masterminding the enslavement of the Ood, has telepathically 'caged' this Hive mind so that it is unable to guide and direct the Ood race. With this and the removal of their hind brain, the Ood's conversion to biological robots is complete.

The term 'robot' is a relatively new word and was coined for the first time in the 1920 play *R.U.R.*, or *Rossum's Universal Robots*, written by Czech playwright Karel Čapek. It comes from the Slavonic word 'robota', meaning 'servitude', 'forced labour' or 'drudgery'. Čapek's play is seen as the birthplace of the modern science fiction robot, but the robots in *R.U.R.* were of biological rather than mechanical manufacture. This was something that the writer felt was an important distinction, and he was dismayed to see his robot's descendants hammered from metal. In his words, 'The world needed mechanical robots, for it believes in machines more than it believes in life.' In Capek's 1920 story the robots eventually realise that they can do without their human masters and rebel. Again, there is that familiar theme, but it is important to put the play into its historical context. The middle classes of the time would have had their own staff of servants; the metaphorical robots of the play represented these servants, and their revolt the anxieties of the Czech middle classes fearing a proletariat Bolshevik uprising. Like Čapek's robots, the androids of Robert Silverberg's *Tower of Glass* (1970) are a form of synthetic human. Manufactured by twenty-forth century entrepreneur-scientist Simeon Krug, they are regarded as property not people. They were a metaphor for slaves, and the novel addresses the issue of slavery in America's history and its subsequent damage to race relations. As can be seen, the robot is very often a useful metaphor for an underclass, allowing an otherwise painful or difficult issue to be examined.

Space-faring humans are not the only race in *Doctor Who* to convert a species into biological robots. One of the best examples of this can be found in *The Dalek Invasion of Earth*. This is the second time the Daleks had appeared in the series, and they are all the more frightening for turning up in an invasion-devastated London. Not to mention that they are busy turning humans into biological robots. Robomen, as they are called, are human males that have been mentally processed to become biological robots to serve the Daleks. They are controlled via special helmets which allow the Daleks to transmit their instructions to them. Although surprisingly adept at hand to hand fighting, the Robomen walk with a zombie-like gait and have a slow-witted manner about them. In a skirmish with well-armed resistance fighters, though, they are fairly easy to defeat, but they are often backed up by the Daleks themselves. The conversion into Robomen is unstable, and after a period of time a Roboman go insane and commit suicide. This means that the Daleks will need to find a continuous supply of prisoners to convert into replacements. Since they have a limited useful lifespan, from a Dalek point of view, they are considered highly expendable. At the same time, the death of a Roboman is signalled via their control helmets to their Daleks masters, and this was a way for the Daleks to locate areas of resistance to be dealt with. It probably isn't in your interest to attack a Roboman.

There were two versions of this story made, the second being a feature film called *Daleks – Invasion Earth: 2150 A.D.* (1966), produced by AARU Productions and staring Peter Cushing as *Doctor Who* and Bernard Cribbins as Tom, a character that fulfils the role of Ian from the TV series. Just as in the original there are Robomen in this story; unlike the TV version, however, they are supplied with what look like standard crash helmets, although with something like a walkie talkie device strapped to the side. Each Roboman is also supplied with shiny black plastic overalls by way of protective clothing. This gives them a very uniform appearance, like some sort of totalitarian state police force. In doing so, however, the film's producers lose much of the horror that comes from seeing a fellow human turned into a mindless machine. Giving them this uniform appearance makes us forget that they had once been individuals. The Robomen in the original version wear civilian clothes, though often with crude Dalek lettering added to emphasise their machine status. The clothing is ragged, a result of wear and tear, and give the Robomen the appearance of tramps. They appear as pathetic and hopeless characters, no longer able to express their personalities through their dress sense because, just like the Ood missing their hindbrains, they no longer have personalities. At the same time, the fact that they are wearing their own clothes also reminds us that these biological machines were once ordinary men with ordinary lives like ours. They had had occupations, ambitions and families. There is a scene where one of the Robomen, whose name had been Phil, kills his brother who had been searching for him. He does this without a glimmer of emotion or recognition, as you might expect from a machine.

In *The War Machines* and *The Green Death* the victims are brainwashed, but the process seems reversible. In *The Dalek Invasion of Earth*, men's brains are altered, their free will is destroyed; there is no going back. There is also some excellent casting of the Robomen and human slaves in the TV production. All are thin; some are gaunt and look convincingly malnourished. All of this makes the idea of invading aliens being able to convert human beings into mindless machines even more chilling.

Frankenstein's creation was, of course, flesh and blood, since he created it from the body parts of human corpses. Because of this his 'monster' is shunned by a society that deems him to be horrific. But there are some people who suggest that we were all created as biological robots. This is a theory promoted by the author Zecharia Sitchin, as part of his ancient astronaut hypothesis. According to him, there are clues hidden in the ancient texts of the Bible and Mesopotamian epics as to the true origins of humanity. According to Sitchin, aliens from the planet 'Nibiru' genetically engineered modern humans from the primitive man apes of the pre-historic earth. This idea is echoed in a *The New Twilight Zone* story from the mid 1980s, called 'A Small Talent for War', in which an alien ambassador comes to Earth and announces that the human race had been genetically engineered by his people. He tells the members of the United Nations Security Council that they are displeased with humanity because they have fallen far short of their potential and that their only real attribute seems to be a 'small talent for war'. In order to avoid Earth's destruction as a failed experiment, the Security Council comes up with a plan to create the perfect peace treaty and so demonstrate humanity's greater potential. Unfortunately, they totally misunderstand the alien ambassador's meaning. The aliens were actually seeking a *greater* talent for war, and had genetically seeded many planets to create suitable warriors to fight their wars for them. Humanity and its small talent is, therefore, of no use to them.

Another biological robot to be found in *Doctor Who* are the Gangers in *The Rebel Flesh* and *The Almost People*. These are made from the 'Flesh' of the first episode's title and manufactured as exact duplicates of their original humans. The 'Flesh' is a programmable matter that begins to learn how to replicate itself at the cellular level and, as the Doctor points out, is therefore living. In a similar way, the robots in *R.U.R* are manufactured from a substance which behaves exactly like living matter, but with a different, more efficient, chemical composition. The robots in *R.U.R.* are manufactured with their own consciousness, but this is not the case with the Gangers. This is so that the original human's consciousness can operate through them, as a kind of expendable work unit to carry out tasks within hazardous areas. Since the process of creating one of these Gangers is relatively quick, their accidental destruction is treated in a very off-hand manner, unlike the loss of a protective suit, which is actually treated with greater concern.

The idea that your consciousness could operate a robot as you are 'wearing' it has been used in science fiction before. The earliest example I can recall was an American science-fiction comic book I read when I was a boy and which featured a story where two human characters arrive on a planet and are seized by robots. They wake to find that they now have robot bodies and that their real bodies are in safe storage. The environment on this particular world is so deadly to humans that the minds of people there have to exist within the bodies of robots, via a consciousness transference, in order to survive. Once they are 'wearing' their robot bodies, they can begin work to find a solution to this poisoned atmosphere. In a variation on this theme, Joe Halderman's novel *The Forever Peace* (1997) features near invincible robots called 'soldierboys' that are operated remotely by people called 'mechanics'. The mechanics' consciousnesses are electronically linked to the robots via an implanted jack in their skulls. The robots are used to fight remotely against third world guerrillas from the comfort and security of the mechanics' home town in the US. This might seem like the perfect solution to having robots that never can rebel against their creators, but there is a twist. When the mechanics are jacked in, they share their consciousness with each other. They begin to change and develop a plan to alter humanity so that there will be everlasting peace, something that their political masters had never imagined.

The film *Blade Runner* (1982), Ridley Scott's cinematic version of Philip K Dick's *Do Androids Dream of Electric*

Sheep?, gives us another example of flesh and blood robots. The Nexus 6 Replicants of Scott's film are at least as intelligent as their designers, have a machine like strength, and are faster and more agile than humans. Since they have no empathy, they are also technically sociopaths. Prior to the events of the film, a Nexus 6 Replicant has already lead a revolt against its human masters in an off world colony, and as a result they are banned from Earth. As a built-in safety measure, they have a life span that is limited to only four years, so while they have adult bodies and high intelligence they are, like Frankenstein's monster, in many ways emotionally like children.

The human within the robot is what makes them such a fascinating subject for us. Usually it is implicit as in *Tower of Glass* or *Blade Runner*, but occasionally the theme is explicit as an artifice openly aspires to become properly human, like the puppet in Carlo Collodi's classic *Pinocchio* (1883). In science fiction this theme is reflected in the film *A.I. Artificial Intelligence* (2001), directed by Steven Spielberg, in which an android with emotions longs to become a real boy. Meanwhile, Issac Asimov's novella *The Bicentennial Man* (1976) and the later film adaptation (1999), directed by Chris Columbus, show a robot who starts to develop 'human' qualities, eventually evolving into a true biological human. The 'ideal' robot, if this is taken to mean a robot without any vestige of humanity, is the model that the Gangers fall short of in *Doctor Who*. They are, apparently empty and soulless vessels, but the Flesh is actually alive, and when the Gangers become self aware as a result of the surge of energy caused by a solar storm, they try to make sense of their bequeathed personalities. As the Doctor points out, 'You poured in your personalities, emotions, traits, memories, secrets, everything. You gave them your lives [...] Are you surprised they walked off with them?' The Gangers are spiritually and emotionally hollow until they are able to retain the personalities that had been placed inside them. In a similar way, the robots of Čapek's *R.U.R.* are initially hollow, without the emotions and drives that complicate human lives. It is only at the insistence of Helena Glory, President of the Humanity League and daughter of President Glory, that the designer of the robots, Dr Gall, attempts to modify the robot design in order to give them souls. It is these modified robots that decide that they are superior to humans and rebel. In the Ganger story the question of them possessing souls is also raised. Cleaves describes the properties of Flesh to the newly arrived Doctor and his companions, relaying how anything can be replicated so that it is identical to the original. The Doctor responds by asking if the mind and soul are included. Later, after the storm has made the Gangers permanent, the Doctor states, 'These are not copies. The storm has hardwired them. They are becoming people.' Jimmy, one of the plant workers, responds, 'With souls?' In both examples the use of the word 'soul' can be considered as meaning that collection of attributes, emotions, drives, personality, which help define us as human. It is the human in both the *R.U.R.* robots and the Gangers that causes them to rebel. They were no longer willing to be considered anything less than beings in their own right.

Scott's Replicants, Silverberg's *Tower of Glass*, The Gangers, Ood and Robomen of *Doctor Who* and the robots from R.U.R. all perform the classic roles of robots and androids in science fiction: attempting to define our humanity. This is especially true of biological robots, whether it is something a robot lacks – a soul – or something that has been taken from them – like the Ood, or the humans of *Invasion Earth* – science fiction asks what it is that makes us human. Does a genetically engineered or mass-produced biological artificial human still qualify as human? Is it our physicality that defines us, or the way we think and feel that really matters? This question of definition becomes explicit in Dan Simmons' *Hyperion* series, where another category of human construct is added to the list, that of the cybrid. These are beings created by combining an AI consciousness, sometimes based on that of a real human historical character, with a specially constructed human body. The body's DNA is human and appearing totally indistinguishable from any other human. As this extract illustrates,

> 'Do you know why people are leery of cybrids?' Hunt asked.
>
> 'Yes,' I said. 'The Frankenstein monster syndrome. Fear of anything in human form that is not completely human. It's the real reason androids were outlawed, I suppose.' 'Uh-huh,' agreed Hunt. 'But cybrids are completely human, aren't they?'

'Genetically they are,' I said. I found myself thinking of my mother, remembering the times I had read to her during her illness. I thought of my brother Tom.

'But they are also part of the Core,' I said, 'and thus fit the description of "not completely human".'[1]

Here we have one of the crucial elements that makes the theme of the human artifice so important in science fiction.

---

[1] Simmons, Dan (2010-11-18). The Fall of Hyperion (GOLLANCZ S.F.) (p. 12). Orion. Kindle Edition.

CHAPTER 4

Isaac Asimov and The Robots of Death!

I started reading about Robot Archie in the *Lion* weekly comic at the age of eight. It wasn't long after that I decided I wanted a robot of my own. Naturally, I put it on my wish list and my grandmother bought it for me the following Christmas.

It was quite a cool-looking robot, with a green translucent body through which could be seen the whirring cogs that made it move. It was powered and controlled via a length of cable from a hand-held unit containing two D size batteries. It reminded me a little of Robby the Robot but I found it to be a rather slow and stupid machine, and it never became the friend and companion that I had hoped for.

Regardless of the shortcomings of my toy, Robot Archie as a character was a force for good, battling supervillains and aliens for the sake of humankind; in this way it reflected one of science fiction's most enduring themes.

Although the technologically created human artifice in science fiction dates back to Mary Shelley's *Frankenstein*, it finally came into its own with the writing of Isaac Asimov's *Robot* stories. This was during the 'golden age' of science fiction, roughly the period 1938 to 1946, which was inspired by widespread conviction that science was a force for human good. The depiction of robots at this time was generally positive, and often they can be read as a metaphor for science in general. However, the advent of weapons of mass destruction, ecological pollution and climate change soon created a mood of mistrust and disillusionment with science and its consequences, bringing this period of science fiction to an end. But Isaac Asimov's *Robot* series, which he began in 1939, testifies to this brief period of optimism in the abilities of humankind to harness the power of science for good.

One of Asimov's many innovations was 'The Three Laws of Robotics', a set of rules hard-wired into the positronic brains (another term he invented) of all his fictional robots, ensuring that they would never turn against their creators.

First Law: A robot may not injure a human being or, through inaction, allow a human being to come to harm.

If a robot is aware of a human being in danger it would be obliged to do whatever it could to help them. There's an example of this in the Asimov inspired film *I, Robot* (2004) where the main protagonist Del Spooner (played by Will Smith) is rescued by a robot from a car that is sinking in a body of water.

The first law means that the robot cannot let Spooner come to harm, it has to do whatever it could to save him.

*

Second Law: A robot must obey the orders given to it by human beings, except where such orders would conflict with the First Law.

The first law governs all other laws, so when the second law states that a robot has to obey the commands of a human being it must not do this if it endangers any other human beings. This is illustrated in the example above.

The accident that threatens to drown Spooner also involves a young girl. The decision to choose which human to save might seem to be an impossible dilemma, but the robot makes a logical decision based on which human is most likely to survive. The robot decides that Spooner has the greatest chance of survival, so puts effort into rescuing him. Spooner's instinct as an adult and a police officer is to sacrifice himself. Spooner therefore orders the robot rescuing him to save the girl. Normally the robot would obey, but it refuses because it calculates that to attempt to rescue the girl would be futile and, in doing so, would mean that Spooner would also die as a result. The robot thus obeys the first law above the second law.

Third Law: A robot must protect its own existence as long as such protection does not conflict with the First or Second Law.

Again using the example above, the robot that rescues Spooner from the sinking car has put itself in danger. Its programming for self preservation is disregarded in order to obey the first law. Were it not for the need to save a human being the robot would have obeyed the third law and not endangered itself.

Despite these checks and balances, Isaac Asimov nevertheless also believed in automatonophobia and predicted that the humans of the future would hold a particular fear of automatons, robots and androids that closely resemble human beings. Asimov called this anxiety the 'Frankenstein Complex' and included it within his stories. He described the public's fear that robots would either replace or come to dominate them. Progress might not seem so appealing when you're the one being made obsolete, particularly when your shiny, new replacement wears a representation of a human face. The overly lifelike, but unnatural, human artifice risks reminding a person of all their shortcomings, whether personal or biological; at best this might just bruise a few egos, but at worst these androids could become a threat to humanity itself. After all, science doesn't just tell us about the world we live in, but our place in it too; if robots and androids can be seen as a metaphor for science, what we learn through them might not always be what we want to hear.

With this in mind, perhaps future intelligent robots should bear as little resemblance to the shape of humans as possible; clunky, functional and clearly designed for servile labour beneath its human masters?

An early appearance of such a type of utility robot was the Mechanoid seen in *The Chase*. The Doctor and his companions encounter them on Mechanus, where the Mechanoids have built a city in preparation for the arrival of human colonists. There is very little 'human' about these robots. In appearance they are large, spherical and made up of triangular panels. They look and behave like machines and produce a series of high frequency sounds which may have been for communication. They are machines built by humans to serve humans, and this is reflected in their appearance.

Despite this, the Mechanoids do not obey the orders of human beings who are not in possession of the correct control codes. As such, Asimov's second law of robotics could only be said to be partially included into their programming. This is something that the Doctor and his human companions quickly fall foul of. Whilst fleeing their Dalek pursuers, they are taken prisoner by the Mechanoids and imprisoned with another human, stranded astronaut Steven Taylor. However, once their captives are in custody, the Mechanoids do nothing to actually physically harm their prisoners, but when the Daleks pursuing the Doctor enter the city they immediately come under attack by the Mechanoids. During the battle the Doctor and his human companions are able to escape.

There was a similar scenario in a short interlude written by John Peel as part of his Eighth Doctor novel *War of the Daleks* (1997), featuring a Mechanoid identified as Mechon 179. Its function was that of a gardener on the planet Hesperus, which, like Mechanoids on Mechanos, is preparing for human colonists. During its work, it is redirected to help defend the new colony from a force of Daleks and is destroyed in the subsequent fighting.

Sadly the Mechanoids never appeared in *Doctor Who*

again; however, in addition to John Peel's novel, they did appear in a number of comic strips and the Big Finish audio drama *The Juggernauts* (2005). In a *TV21* comic strip 'The Daleks', later called 'The Dalek Chronicles', they were depicted as a self-governing race of mechanical beings, with no reference being given to their human creators. Interestingly, when the Emperor Dalek is presenting the results of an analysis of them, he describes them as having a 'positronic brain.'

Is it a function of their un-humanlike design that seems to make these Mechanoids less threatening to us? They were built to serve humans and even when they function as independent beings they behave benignly towards humans, in contrast to their behaviour towards the Daleks. Their 'built-to-serve' design and purpose lends itself to being a less threatening 'species' of manmade robot.

In contrast, the robots in *The Robots of Death* are based on the human form. The human crew of a gigantic Sandminer vehicle, Storm Mine 4, are being murdered, and it appears that one or more of the Sandminer's complement of android robots is doing the killing. The robots in *Robots of Death* are very distinctive, with their art deco design, finesse and well-mannered voices. They lack body language, fingerprints, DNA and had a uniformity of appearance that make them very chilling serial killers. They are non-human humanoids that are perfect candidates for Asimov's Frankenstein complex. We associate machines with mass production and consistent appearance, so uniformity of appearance seems to be a recurring theme with robots. But it isn't just mechanical robots that seem to have uniformity. The Robomen in *Daleks – Invasion Earth: 2150 A.D.* (1966) wear identical helmets, reflective goggles (so obscuring most of their face) and shiny black plastic overalls that also give them a very uniform appearance. They are humans made to look like mass produced machines. The Sandminer robots, despite efforts to make them resemble humans, *are* mass produced machines. In both cases our minds are likely to 'rebel' at this false image of humanity.

The robots from *The Robots of Death* are 'Asimov' robots, programmed never to harm humans, but they are corrupted by a mad scientist (there's another one!) called Taren Capel, who has grown up with robots, somehow becoming psychotically bonded with them in the process. (You might notice that the name of this villain is homage to robot folklore's Karel Čapek, the writer of *R.U.R.*). Somehow he has been able to override the robots' programming, enabling them to kill humans. His utopian dream is to create a society free of humans for himself and his robot 'brothers'. So much does he identify with robots that, towards the end of the story, he even colours his skin and dresses to look like one. Growing up with robots, this brilliant man would have learned that they were courteous, caring and self sacrificing, unable to lie and never resentful, jealous or spiteful. He may well have grown to see these companions as something superior to aspire towards. The robots exhibited all our best qualities and none of our faults. Their influence on a young boy who had little contact with other human beings might have been to create unrealistic expectations of human relationships, but once thrust out into a world of self-centred humans that included back-stabbers, cheats, liars and frauds the sudden contrast must have made him recoil from his humanity and cause him to want to be something better; a robot in fact. In effect Capel wants to become a creature of science, symbolically putting all his faith in it and so losing touch with his humanity. This imbalance drives him insane and it has to be said, he becomes a right nutter, but brilliant nevertheless.

No matter how hard we try to make a robot look like a human being it will never be able to interact with us the way that human beings do. In fact this inability may make androids more unsettling the more like humans they appear. There is one illustration of how a human society incorporating robots could work very successfully in Iain M Banks Culture series of science fiction novels. The artificially intelligent machines, 'Minds' and 'Drones', have an equal status to humans and other biological alien species that inhabit the Culture. The super intelligent 'Minds' have the responsibility of its governance and their abilities complement humanity's in such a way as to bring out the best of us. The robotic 'Drones' have designs which are infinitely variable and do not mimic the human form, instead of arms and legs they make use of invisible force fields to move and manipulate objects. They are obvious machines, so do not create the unease that something which appears as human would cause. Interestingly the Drones have their own body language that is also understood by all the biological citizens of the Culture. This is based on visible, coloured fields of patterned colours called 'auras', through which they express their emotions.

One of the really great things about *The Robots of Death* was that it incorporated some of the then-current research on body language into the plot. Human beings don't just communicate with words. Body language is an important part of the way we communicate at a subconscious level: posture, facial expressions, how we move and the subtle scents we produce. This evolved before we developed verbal language and is an important form of animal communication. How would we react to humanoid machines that didn't exhibit body language, something that we depend on so much (even though we may not realise it)? There had been a research paper produced shortly before the programme aired suggesting that women were more adept at reading body language then men. This is why a woman might often accuse a man of shouting at her in an argument even though he is keeping his voice low. It is his body language that is shouting at her! *The Robots of Death* tips its hat to this discovery through the Doctor's companion Leela: on-board the Sandminer is an undercover detective called Poul and his robot partner D84 (the D standing for Dumb), an undercover Super Voc, and it is Leela who points out that Poul 'walks like a hunter', the first hint in the story that he is not what he seems.

The second, and from the point of view of human interaction with robots, more interesting use of body language in the story is the way that Poul, who depends so much on reading body language in his detecting work, reacts when he discovers that the murderer is a robot. His mind can't handle the fact and he has a breakdown as a result. Poul has no doubt grown up convinced that robots were a predictable, consistent and benign technology. The realisation that they have become capable of murder must come as a severe shock to everything he believes in. He feels well-equipped to deal with criminal human beings but totally defenceless, defeated even, by the prospect of a technology that was no longer benign or predictable. The Doctor describes his withdrawn, terrified state as 'Grimwade's Syndrome', a form of robophobia, but that doesn't really do justice to what Poul is going through; a complete loss of faith in human technology.

The Robots of Death illustrated something about robots and androids I hadn't really thought of before. There are potential psychological problems when human beings interact with robots and androids that are unable to communicate with body language.

As a result of losing Poul, his human partner, D84 has to team up with the Doctor to solve the case. As this new working relationship begins, a yearning hope was kindled within me that D84 would go on to become a permanent companion to the Doctor. These were dashed when he was unnecessarily (in my opinion) killed off at the end of the story. He was one of the best companions the Doctor never had, and I found out later that there had been plans for him to join the Doctor, but these were scrapped in favour of a robot in the shape of a small dog! I was so irked by this poor decision making by the production team that I sent a proposal to BBC Worldwide for a *Doctor Who* novel that brought back D84. Unfortunately, the BBC's decision making hadn't improved in the interim. Nevertheless, *The Robots of Death* is one of my favourite *Doctor Who* stories. It was written by people who were well versed in robot fiction, incorporating themes from Asimov's writing and adding well-thought-out elements of their own. The design and direction of the production, particularly the design of the robots, was inspired. I can even forgive them using rear bicycle reflectors as 'corpse markers' – the indicators placed onto deactivated damaged robots awaiting repair.

Contrast this with a more recent story *Voyage of the Damned*. To be strictly accurate, this should be considered an alien robots story, but the human characters, style of retro Earth clothing and the space liner mimicking the SS Titanic (whoever thought that that would be a good idea?) suggest that its creators modelled it on a possible future humanity story. The robots in this story are known as Hosts and are dressed as Christmas tree angels, no doubt to help us get into the mood for the holiday season and at the same time reinforce the feeling that the action is taking place in a future human society. The function of these robots is to aid the paying passengers by providing information as and when required, but the only significant element they add to the story is as an additional threat to the Doctor and his party. The episode's greatest achievement is that of being one of the most obvious works of 'skiffy' I have ever seen. Skiffy is derived from the abbreviation sci-fi and is a term used by the more serious science fiction fans to describe a mainstream story that has been given the location and trappings of science fiction without any of the ideas that really make the genre. The episode contained a number of elements from some classic disaster stories, *The Poseidon Adventure* (1972), *Towering Inferno* (1974), *Voyage of The Damned* (1976) and *Titanic* (1997) together with *Goldfinger* (1964) then mixed these together and projected the result out into space with a few added aliens and a mob of renegade robots.

The robots in *The Robots of Death* were Asimov robots, and the humans involved in the events that took place on the Sandminer could barely comprehend the possibility that some of their robots had become killers. When they finally did, a few began to descend into paranoia and madness. But in *Voyage of the Damned*, not one character seems to find it incomprehensible that the robots have turned on them! The villain is a nutter capitalist with a personal score to settle; he also happens to be a cyborg, and his henchmen a bunch of robots in the guise of angels. Having a capitalist who is good at bypassing robot safeguards is less convincing than a renowned, if insane, scientist whose speciality is robotics. And defining the villain as a cyborg does not make the story science fiction. It is the ideas about the relationship between technology and culture that do that, and I didn't see much in this story. *The Robots of Death* asks an interesting question about how technology interacts with culture, and if any level of safeguards is enough for a potentially dangerous technology, something that applies as much to nuclear power stations as it does to robots and androids.

This story even manages to get some of the basic science wrong as we are presented with three flaming meteors in the vacuum of space. It is the friction caused by their entry into the atmosphere that makes them flaming, in the vacuum of space they are just lumps of iron and rock. Maybe that was a bit of poetic license, but I do dislike misinformation.

This story instead is a social commentary, not about how society reacts to science and technology, but more about the social prejudices and arrogance of capitalism. It is a story rich in metaphors. At one point Astrid says to the cyborg Bannakaffalatta, 'Cyborgs are getting equal rights. They passed a law back on Sto. You can even get married.'

She could well be talking about the changes in our own society, by allowing same sex couples to marry. Later when confronted by the Doctor, the villain orchestrating the disaster, Capricorn, partly justifies his actions by saying, '[…] in a society that despises cyborgs. I've had to hide away for years, running the company by hologram.'

He could also be referring to the long held prejudices, forcing gay men and women to project a false persona in order to be allowed to work and live within society. There are also illustrations of prejudice against overweight people and examples of the contempt rich people have for those less fortunate than themselves. The engineered attempt to crash the space liner could even be seen as a metaphor for greedy and selfish capitalists willing to torpedo an economy, destroying the livelihoods of so many innocent people, if it will get them a bigger bonus or a better pension plan. This is the sort of writing Russell T Davies does so well, but the science and technology in this story amounts to many MacGuffins[1] that create a series of goals the Doctor and his charges have to achieve to bring the story to a successful conclusion. The Hosts turn bad with no discernible safeguards to have prevented this from happening, something that seems incredibly short-sighted of the culture that created them. At each encounter with the Host the Doctor and his charges have to find a way past or away from them. Automatonophobia, or any concern that society has become dependent on them, is not an issue. They are not used in the kitchens or for serving drinks. If there is a reason for this, it is not explained. Their wings are not just decorative, but functional. Why this would be necessary of an interstellar ocean liner is also not explained, but it turns out to be useful for the plot, both in creating opportunities for threat and working towards the successful conclusion. Making the Host masculine figures may also have been intended to increase their sense of threat. However, it occurs to me that if they had been created as female, the contrast between them as angelic helpers and hunter killers would have been far greater and more disturbing. The Hosts are, in fact, Christmas decorations that become deadly – a reoccurring theme in the seasonal specials.

Critics praised *Voyage of the Damned*, something justified by its position as number two in the Christmas TV ratings. The story had outstanding visual qualities and entertained

---

[1] A **MacGuffin** (aka McGuffin or maguffin) is an object, event, or character that is typically unimportant to the overall plot, but is there to set and keep the plot in motion

for over an hour on Christmas Day. But whilst *Voyage of the Damned* was a hit, it was only pretending to be science fiction.

If you're going to put robots in science fiction stories, you have to do something a little more original than have them wander around being homicidal. They need to fulfil a role of asking questions about us as human beings, and our technology. An excellent example of this is a film called *The Machine* (2013). It has a tag line, 'They Rise, We Fall', which hints at a scenario we have seen before in films such as *Terminator* (1984). But to expect another tale of robot insurrection would be a mistake. This is more a film about evolution than it is about machine revolution. True, there is enough use of automatic weapons and explosions to satisfy anyone expecting such things, but director and writer Caradog W James's nuanced tone of subtlety take us away from many of the modern clichés of the Robot film genre. The film hints back to Mary Shelly's *Frankenstein*, but unlike Victor Frankenstein, the creator of this human artifice, a scientist called Vincent McCarthy shows humanity towards his creation, something that is returned in spades. Robots and androids are often depicted in science fiction as cold and logical creations. Humans, with their emotions and conscience, are in contrast depicted as superior. The refreshing thing about *The Machine* is that it is the humans and their institutions that are cold, logical and lacking emotion and conscience. This film is an intelligent and entertaining exploration of the subject of artificial intelligence that doesn't resort to formula. It is not the robot that has malfunctioned or been corrupted, but the human institutions of government that are corrupt. There is no mad scientist turning good robots to evil purposes, but institutional science in the service of the government that is attempting to do so.

A *Doctor Who* story that featured robots but avoided the nutter-turning-them-bad cliché is *The Girl Who Waited*. The Doctor's companion, Amy, becomes trapped in a separate time stream whilst visiting a Kindness Centre on the planet Apalapucia. The Kindness Centre's medical staff are robots called Handbots. Again, strictly speaking, these are alien robots, but they do represent a very likely development for human-made robots. After military and industrial applications, the most likely and appropriate application of robot technology would be in the field of health care. With an ageing population, there would be a desperate need for carers that had suitable dietary and medical knowledge whilst also being capable of providing companionship and mental stimulation. This is the premise of the film *Robot & Frank* (2012), which is set in the near future and features an ageing cat-burglar suffering from dementia, and his care worker robot. Because of the complexities of looking after a failing human body and mind, the robot needs a high degree of intelligence and the ability to carry out household tasks. The Handbots in *The Girl Who Waited* have limited intelligence and are unable to identify different species of humanoids or diagnose the correct medication for their charges. Their only function seems to be to administer a single drug, developed to counteract the effects of a plague called Chen7. Indeed, the Kindness Centres themselves were created purely for the sufferers of this plague, so its creators might be forgiven for assuming that only legitimate patients would reside in them. It seems logical, therefore, that the simplistic Handbots were mass-produced specifically for the purpose of administering a single drug in these centres. But given that the Apalapucians' level of technology included teleporting, it seems a little odd that they didn't make their robots more intelligent. Maybe their safeguard against renegade robots was to deliberately limit their intelligence? If this was the case, it does beg the question; might it not have been more efficient for the patients in the centre to be prompted by the interface to go to a fixed, computer controlled drug dispenser when required?

Making the Handbots simplistic allowed them to be used as a threat within the episode, even though they had been constructed to be benign. There were no safeguards to prevent them harming someone, albeit accidentally. They could have been monitored and controlled by the interface, which would have been able to give them fresh instructions as and when required. In this way, unforeseen circumstances could have been catered for. To this story's credit, it did attempt to use the robots as a threat that didn't involve their safeguards being subverted. They operated exactly as they were intended to, all the time thinking they were performing their duties correctly. No doubt they would not have harmed any humanoid had they realised they were doing so.

There just happened to be huge gaps in the Kindness Centre's safety mechanisms and procedures, allowing them to kill with kindness. But perhaps the writer of *The Girl Who Waited* is asking a very interesting question about robots and their design. The world that a robot can see and the way that it sees it are defined by its human designers who will model this perception on their own. Isn't it possible therefore that we could create machines that conforms to our oversights and mistakes? The creators of the Kindness Centre failed to consider that anyone who wasn't a sufferer of Chen7 could ever be included in its walls. They designed the robots with this perception, that only Chen7 sufferers would be encountered by them. The robots behaved faultlessly, but their understanding of the universe around them had been skewed, mirroring the mistaken perceptions of their biological creators. This is in fact a very plausible and original idea when considering robots and the dangers they present. Perhaps future robot designers should take heed.

The human artifice in science fiction serves as a metaphor for our social or technological anxieties. The murder mysteries of Agatha Christie are given a new twist when the murderer is an Asimov robot in *The Robots of Death*. Machines made in our image reflect our concerns about the nature of humanity. But, as *In The Girl Who Waited*, if our view of the universe is biased, blinkered, or short-sighted can we expect our machines to be any better? Science fiction has from its very beginnings been concerned with the interaction of the human and the technological. This interaction has alternately expressed both our fears and our hopes. Asimov presented us with robots that were benign, others have given us the flipside. The robot in science fiction is both an expression of our technological fears and hopes and an attempt to measure what is human. Perhaps we are happier when that technology does not remind us of ourselves, because ultimately that is what we fear. The powerful technology that we create may become a mirror of our worst faults and might be what destroys us at last.

CHAPTER 5
Robots from Other Worlds

Asimov predicted humans and androids working as partners, and we saw an example of this in *The Robots of Death* with the partnership of the human investigator Poul and the robot D84. In *The Day the Earth Stood Still* the partnership is between the alien Klaatu and Gort.

It was during 1971 while Jon Pertwee was battling aliens in *The Dæmons* that I came home one evening to find my parents watching *The Day the Earth Stood Still*. I had been enjoying the, relatively new, novelty of being able to buy alcoholic beverages in the pub with some of my friends and was still developing my tolerances for bitter. My perception of the film was probably, therefore, a little skewed. It was towards the end of the story and Gort, the robot that was the alien emissary Klaatu's bodyguard and assistant, is in the process of rescuing the body of his master. Gort is unstoppable, firing death rays from beneath his visor and vaporising anything in his path. Having recovered the body of Klaatu he gently carries him back to their saucer where he revives him so that he can give the people of Earth a final warning and message of hope. Possibly because of my slight lack of sobriety it all seemed very profound to me. What was more, I found myself longing for a Gort of my own.

That desire for a robot friend and companion hadn't gone away.

Bodyguards and Assistants

Alien robot assistants and bodyguards appear in *Doctor Who* as well. The android in *The Visitation* is a bodyguard for the reptilian Terileptil shipwrecked on Earth during the seventeenth century. This group of Terileptil are a particularly bad bunch of escaped convicts that are both ruthless and desperate to avoid being sent back to serve the rest of their hard labour in the tinclavic mines on Raaga. Their escape pod crashes near the location of the future Heathrow airport and shortly afterwards the Terileptil convicts invade a local Manor house that is vigorously defended by its owners. One of the Terileptil is fatally wounded by a flintlock pistol and it is only the arrival of the aliens' robot that guarantees their victory. Despite their futuristic weapons they need the robot for protection and to carry out tasks too dangerous for them to undertake themselves. The Doctor acknowledges this fact when he says, 'The androids are programmed to protect. The only way around them is to destroy them before they destroy you.'

Perhaps the only thing more chilling than a human manufactured robot gone wrong are ones belonging to aliens that are full of evil intent and not to be reasoned with and their service to their masters can be manifested in a number of ways.

It is interesting that the robot is modelled more on the

human form than that of the Terileptil. It has a face which mimics the eyes nose and mouth of something resembling a human being. Since it is likely that an alien species would model their robots on themselves, the way we humans endeavour to do, it seems logical to assume that the Terileptil's robot is a product of another species and was 'acquired' by them. In fact the leader of the Terileptil group suggests as much when he says, '...we can travel the universe and acquire androids.' They have obtained this robot as some might a slave.

The Terileptil plan is to exterminate the human race with a strain of super plague and then use androids to create their paradise on Earth. They have rejected the idea of merely enslaving human beings, preferring to have an army of robots slaves instead. This echoes the lament of Karel Čapek when he says, 'The world needed mechanical robots, for it believes in machines more than it believes in life.' This seems to be true of the Terileptil who would rather have machine slaves than living ones. The Terileptil convicts care little for other living beings and they put their trust in the predictable and obedient robot machines, which they buy or steal accordingly. We can see that the sort of robot or android an alien species uses tells us a great deal about their character and attitudes.

It is one of the Doctor's companions, Nyssa, who succeeds in destroying the robot, but she is far from happy in doing so: 'It was such a magnificent machine […] It was a slave. It was only doing what it was told.' For her, it seems that merely being mechanical does not preclude something from being alive.

The robot in the *The Sontaran Experiment* is a relatively unsophisticated looking device, resembling more the robots we currently send to places like Mars. In fact this Sontaran robot performs a parallel function as it scouts around the post-solar flare devastated Earth looking for sample humans to capture for Field Major Styre's cruel experiments. I remember being thoroughly unimpressed by this machine which hardly registered as a robot. Yet it reflected the character of the Sontarans perfectly; basic, utilitarian, unaesthetic. The Sontarans are all about war and nothing but war and, as a result, they build machines fit for this purpose and nothing more. In contrast, the android in *The Visitation* is created with artistic flair and imagination. Its creators put something of themselves into it so that it is not just a machine, but something of a work of art to reflect their tastes and nature. The Sontaran machine has none of these qualities because the Sontarans themselves do not possess them. Field Major Styre and the Sontaran Marshal lacked the imagination required to know that they were being fooled by the Doctor. Perhaps this was their greatest weakness.

Dead Robots Walking

Pyramids of Mars creates a believable alien species, known as the Osirians, who have become the basis of ancient Egyptian mythology. The last survivor of the Osirians is Sutekh (also known as Set) who is believed to be the god of storms, the desert, and chaos. In this story we see what the Earth will look like in 1980 if Sutekh isn't defeated. It is reduced to a desolate and lifeless desert in perpetual storm. Sutekh destroyed his own planet, Phaester Osiris and then left a trail of destruction across the galaxy as he was pursued by his brother, Horus and the surviving Osirians, finally being caught and defeated on Earth. He was imprisoned in a subterranean tomb beneath a blind pyramid in Egypt. His imprisonment was sustained by an enabling signal sent from Mars, a sort of interplanetary key. Destroying the source of the signal would release Sutekh, causing him to wreak havoc on Earth and beyond.

It is archaeologist Marcus Scarman entering his prison that gives Sutekh an opportunity to attempt an escape. Marcus Scarman is converted into a biological robot to facilitate his plans. Amongst his tasks is the transportation of equipment to his home in England for the operation; including a number of robots whose appearance mimic that of Egyptian mummies.

The Osirian service robots are neither good nor bad, but simply obedient. They are intelligent enough to understand verbal orders and adapt to the unexpected, but nothing more. In *Pyramids of Mars* one robot becomes ensnared in a man-trap and only after several minutes of futile attempts to walk away does it finally stop to analyse the problem and free itself. They are built to provide raw labour with no capacity for moral judgements. Nor do they carry any exotic weapons and kill by simply using their enormous physical strength. Towards the end of the story we see a number of these robots in the service of Horus.

They have been left to guard The Eye of Horus; the source of the signal inside the Pyramid on Mars. The only distinguishing feature they have is gold binding worn around their chest and shoulders. A robot guarding the Eye engages in combat with a robot sent by Sutekh. This amounts to each of them trying to bash the other into destruction. Horus, it seems, has not left any more sophisticated robots on Mars. Perhaps those had been left with the Osirians. Or is it more likely that the Osirians did not need sophisticated robots because of their advanced psychic and mental powers. Like the Krell, they are able to manipulate energy with their mind so preferring to keep their robots to the level of useful machines. In doing so they avoid any possible rebellions. This could well be an indication of their wisdom, experiences, or both! They seem to be a species on the verge of outgrowing their robots completely.

Robots in Armour

Aliens using robots and androids as bodyguards and assistants is one thing, but it becomes a lot more frightening when robots are used en masse, like in an invasion or rebellion for example. The Gundans are robots featured in *Warriors' Gate*. They had been built by slaves to lead the revolt against their masters; the time-sensitive Tharil. Their purpose is to kill Tharils, and like their intended victims the Gundans can travel the time winds to hunt them down. The appearance of the Gundan is like that of a medieval knight, with full plate armour. They carry an axe as a weapon and their helmets are decorated with horns to make them seem more frightening. The face of the robot, behind the mesh of the helmet's visor, is reminiscent of a skull, or Death's Head, adding to their terror. It seems important for any downtrodden people to terrorise those they deem responsible for their oppression. It isn't enough for the slaves of the Tharils to liberate themselves, or even kill their masters. They need them to feel dread and terror before they die and so they design their robots accordingly.

The Doctor finds several energy-depleted dormant Gundans when he visits the feasting hall in the gateway between the universes. Like ornamental suits of armour in some medieval banqueting chamber, they adorn the perimeter of the feasting table at which many of the skeletons of their victims remain. Predictably, in classic horror tradition, first one and then another of the Gundans reanimate themselves. With nearly depleted energy cells they move slowly, with a zombie-like gait, reminding us of the undead. Perhaps that is what they are after all; not living creatures, but not dead either. They have no conscience, no inhibitions, only a purpose and that is to hack terrified Tharils to death in a brutally medieval way.

There is a slave freighter in the story commanded by Rorvik who has an air of a pompous Captain Mainwaring about him without any of the latter's redeeming features. Rather he is as sadistic and ruthless as any SS officer. In fact the actor who played Rorvik, Clifford Rose, also played SS Sturmbannführer Ludwig Kessler in the late 1970s highly acclaimed BBC series *Secret Army*. Much of that character comes forth in Rorvik. His crew are a mishmash of uninspired characters seeming to lack any moral fibre, but then you might expect that from the crew of a slave ship. The idea of using an enslaved time-sensitive Tharil to navigate a star ship is an interesting one. It echoes the navigators of the Spacing Guild in Frank Herbert's science fiction novel *Dune* (1965) later made into a film in 1984 and a TV series in 2003. Within the Imperium of Dune all computers have been outlawed and there are references in the novel to a war, known as the The Butlerian Jihad, with sentient machines. Spacecraft, therefore, have to be navigated through deep space by selectively evolved prescient humans called Navigators who rely on the 'spice' melange to facilitate their mental abilities.

The first time I saw it I found the story uncomfortably claustrophobic. It had the feel and quality of an unpleasant dream one couldn't wake up from. This made me empathise with the characters trapped within the shrinking microcosmic universe of the plot. It is a story that is well worth revisiting, intriguing on many levels and even humorous at times. It reverses the role of the Tharils from master to slave, suggesting that two wrongs don't make a right, and holds up very well as a standalone story although it is part of the E-Space trilogy. The Gundans have the feel of robots from a bygone age whose purpose has been served. The remaining examples seem like so much flotsam and jetsam left in the stream of history. More than anything they remain a physical manifestation of an oppressed people's intense anger, hatred and desire for vengeance, and their continence reflected this perfectly.

There was another robot created to look like an armoured knight in *The Time Warrior*. A Sontaran named Linx becomes stranded in thirteenth century medieval England and falls in with a robber baron named Irongron. Linx begins supplying him with anachronistic weapons with which to attack his neighbours' castles. In addition to rifles, Linx builds Irongron a robot made to look like an armoured knight with a promise to build him an army of them. The robot is not as sophisticated as the Gundans. It has a stiff awkward gait, limited arm movement and requires a control box to operate it, something that Irongron seems to master surprisingly quickly. It didn't seem very much more advanced than the robot my grandmother had bought me, except that there was no external power supply, it had a better sense of balance and (it has to be said) it was a lot quicker. Sontarans prefer to fight their own battles and would treat the suggestion that they might have robots fight their battles for them with disdain. Link's gift might seem a little odd therefore, even if given to an 'inferior species' like medieval humans. Irongron's greatest need in conquering the world and building an empire (ambitions that a Sontaran like Linx could relate to) was a shortage of manpower, and manpower of good quality at that. As he says, 'With a few such soldiers as that, I could take the world!' Sontarans had overcome this problem by cloning themselves in vast numbers. The human reproductive system was 'inefficient' and not conducive to building armies or quickly replacing casualties. The next best thing, from a Sontaran's point of view, might well be the mass production of warriors in robot form, at least until Irongron's descendants could develop the superior cloning technology.

Something that compromised the production's design of Linx's robot in the story was the fact that the actor's costume required the head to be knocked off. The result was something that moved and fought in such an awkward and unnatural way that it was almost comical. A similar design to that of the Gundans would have been so much more realistic and threatening and the head being knocked off could have been handled with some judicious cuts and edits (no pun intended).

This idea of robots disguised as medieval knights reoccurs in *Robot of Sherwood*. Again we have a scenario of aliens crashing in medieval England and then falling in with a local despot to repair their craft. The aliens in this case though are robots from twenty-ninth century Earth travelling to the Promised Land[1] in an age when knights were travelling to and from the Holy Land and something that could have been made more of. These robots are able to adapt their appearance to look like a uniform order of knights and their spacecraft like Nottingham Castle, based on information stored in their database. Like the alien robot Gort their visors open to reveal a metallic humanoid face from which is fired a deadly laser ray capable of turning any human into a pile of dust. Given the special effects of the twenty-first century production they looked convincing, though frustratingly we learn very little about them. Why were they travelling on their own, without human

---

[1] Part of a story arc for the Twelfth Doctor's first series

supervision? Had they rebelled and escaped or been sent on a hazardous mission from which they were subverted into their quest for the Promised Land? In this story, as in so many of the twenty-first century production stories, robots were simply being used as a convenient menace. A pity, because they were such beautifully crafted robots they deserved a multiple episode story.

Robot Foot Soldiers

A common use for alien robots in *Doctor Who* is as foot soldiers, particularly when invading another planet. One invasion that barely deserves to be called such occurred in *The Dominators*. Two aliens, the eponymous Dominators, arrive on the planet Dulkis and, more or less, declare it conquered. To back this up they have a force of diminutive robots called Quarks. They are the foot soldiers of the Dominators; literally since they walk about on little feet armed with a devastating energy weapon. They are much more than just this however, since it transpires that they are the Swiss Army knife of robots. Even their multiple arms suggest this; one pair folds into the body, the other pair retracts. They also act as a form of power pack on legs. The Quarks are required to power the drilling device which will be used to facilitate the planet Dulkis being turned into a vast molten ball of radioactivity, providing the Dominator war fleet with its required energy source. This explains why Navigator Rago, the senior Dominator, becomes so agitated when Probationer Toba, who is something of a homicidal maniac, wastes much of their limited energy reserves to destroy and kill at the least provocation. Even with their Quarks the Dominators would have found it difficult to operate were it not for the fact that the Dulcians had enjoyed several generations of pacifism. Apart from some functioning museum pieces they have no weapons. More importantly they have trouble even conceptualising the process of war, something that is emphasised by the male Dulcians habit of wearing dresses made out of what look like curtains. The Dominators are like wolves let lose amongst a flock of sheep and it is up to the Doctor and his companions to play the part of guarding sheepdogs. Only one Dulcian is willing and able to offer any resistance. Cully is something of a throwback and misfit in Dulcian society, seeking stimulation and adventure by committing various misdemeanours. He seems to have the ability to fight back, where his fellows cannot.

The Dominators deserve some closer examination. Their appearance is somehow reminiscent of Frankenstein's monster (minus scars and stitching). They are tall and their costumes suggest high broad shoulders. They also speak in a machine like manner to each other. When Rago admonishes Toba for destroying a Dulcian vessel he uses a very precise phrasing, 'You are a Probationer Navigator. Your first task is to investigate, second assess. You allowed your instinct for destruction to interfere with your primary task.' More importantly, perhaps, these two Dominators seem to lack any empathy, humour, creativity or pity. In fact they seem only to have those emotions that will enable them to be pragmatic and ruthless soldiers. Watching them I am reminded again of *The New Twilight Zone* story called *A Small Talent for War* mentioned in Chapter 3. Could they have been a product of a genetic modification program? Are they themselves a form of biological robot? It would explain a great deal about their character. Seen in this way the Quarks become more of an accessory to the biological robot Dominators, an extension of their capabilities. The two Dominators carry no weapons themselves, but rely totally on the Quarks for defensive and offensive capabilities. They are like one half of a biological/synthetic robot team.

The Quarks have been a much underrated robot. The idea that a robot could be designed to be used as a mobile power pack to operate various bits of equipment, rather the way a farmer's tractor does, is original. They are both cute with their diminutive size and squeaky childlike voices, and deadly, so creating a conflict in our minds. In a better story they might have become one of the icons of *Doctor Who*.

Not all aliens or their robots are bad, of course. The Chumblies in *Galaxy 4* were the robots of hideous, ammonia-breathing aliens called the Rill. However, it turned out that the Rill were the good guys, being friendly and compassionate and, like the Doctor, primarily interested in exploring the universe. Their antagonists, the Drahvins, on the other hand, were beautiful blonde female humanoids, consisting of low-intelligence cloned soldiers (arguably biological robots) and their aggressive leader, Maaga. She was treacherous and oppressive and only interested in making war. In a peculiar way they had a lot in common with the Sontarans. It was refreshing to see a *Doctor Who* story where the implied message was not to judge by appearances. To paraphrase Sam Gamgee from *Lord of the Rings*, the Rill looked foul, but felt fair.

When the Doctor's companion, Vicki, first sees one of the Rills' robots she names it a Chumbley because of the sound it makes when it moves along. Whether the Rill had a name for their robots is never revealed, but they seem to like Vicki's suggestion and begin using the name themselves. As a telepathic species the Rill need to be able to communicate with non-telepathic aliens. The Chumblies facilitate this communication by vocalising the thoughts of their Rill masters. As ammonia-breathers the Rill are also limited in their ability to explore oxygen rich planets and use the Chumblies to probe and explore, very much like we might explore the deep oceans or an alien planet in our solar system with a robotic prob.

The Chumblies have weapons, but only use them as a last resort. When attacked they often simply 'hunker down' the concentric shells of their metal bodies, collapsing down into each other and presenting nothing but a protective shell to their enemies. They are cute little droids, emphasising the good nature of their masters.

Although alien robots in *Doctor Who* arguably represent many of the same fears and anxieties as their human-made cousins, there are some distinct differences. As human-created robots focus our minds on what makes us human, the role of the alien robot should be to emphasise that which is alien. While alien robots in *Doctor Who* represent many of the same fear and anxieties as their human-made cousins, there are some distinct differences. As humans we only have ourselves to compare with and may project our most disagreeable faults onto such threats and personify them, but the alien-made robots in *Doctor Who* indicate much about the aliens themselves. As human-created robots reflect human characteristics and focus our mind on what makes us human, the alien robots should emphasise what it is to be alien. As we saw in Chapter 4 robots can represent science and technology, either as a force for good or evil. Alien robots can, therefore, represent the threat of a superior technology we cannot match. In the sixties the idea of a robot of any sort would have seemed very advanced, and this was reflected in the science fiction of the time. The general consensus was that one key indicator of a species' technological sophistication might well be if they *had* robots or not. That, of course, was an extrapolation of the current technology of the time. Now producers have so much more to extrapolate from, nano technology, cloning, cell manipulation and genetic modification, the Internet, quantum mechanics including the relationship between matter and energy, space time and the multiverse to name but a few. To quote Sir Arthur Stanley Eddington, British astronomer, physicist, and mathematician of the early twentieth century, 'Not only is the universe stranger than we imagine – it is stranger than we can imagine.'

CHAPTER 6
Servitors of the Great Old Ones

Yeti, Snowmen, Spoonheads and Whispermen of the Great Intelligence

As a young boy I attended a convent school where I was taught, as an undeniable truth, that at the end of the world we would all give up our corporeal bodies to live as spiritual beings. None of this was based on science of course, but science fiction author Arthur C Clarke used this idea as the basis of what is considered to be one of his best novels, *Childhood's End*. An alien race, known as the Overlords, facilitate the transcendence of humanity from corporeal existence to one that can best be compared to something spiritual or godlike. This was also the underlying theme of the film and novel, *2001: A Space Odyssey* in which unseen aliens select mankind as suitable candidates for eventual transcendent evolution.

Arthur C Clarke makes the assumption that achieving an existence as a disembodied entity is a desirable state, something that is challenged by the behaviour of one particular enemy of the Doctor, the Great Intelligence, which first featured in *The Abominable Snowmen*. Contrary to the trend defined by Arthur C Clarke, the aim of the Great

Intelligence was the creation a body for itself with which it could conquer planet Earth. The development of this enemy of the Doctor owes much to the works of HP Lovecraft, an American author who is often classified as horror. Lovecraft's stories describe aliens that are so strange and powerful that they appear as demons and gods to us mere mortal humans. One of these aliens called Yog-Sothoth is a member of a race known simply as the Great Old Ones, a catch-all name for any alien species that have survived the end of the preceding universe and passed into our own. It is often depicted as a mass of spheres. The back story for the Great Intelligence suggests it is based on Lovecraft's creation. At every encounter between the Doctor and the Great Intelligence the alien has been aided by automatons of various sorts and because it spans such a great period of time, between its first appearance in September 1967 to its final one in May 2013, it allows us to examine the evolution of these automatons, both from a stylistic and thematic point of view.

In *The Abominable Snowmen* the Great Intelligence takes possession of High Lama Padmasamabhava and uses him to build a force of robots in the shape of the cryptozoological Yeti. Within the Himalayas these robots function appropriately enough, confusing and frightening away observers and, when required, operating as an attack force. A later appearance in *The Web of Fear* sees these Yeti occupy London's underground system. The logic for them maintaining this disguise is never explained other than that examples of these robots are brought back to London as curiosities by Professor Travers. Presumably, once reactivated they are able to duplicate themselves into greater numbers. The design has evolved to something the Doctor describes as a Mark II version, so explaining their new ability to roar and light their eyes when attacking, adding to their fearsome aspect. Ineffectively combating these robots are elements of the British Army initially led by Captain Knight and then by Colonel Lethbridge-Stewart. In combat the Yeti operated rather like tanks, approaching and overwhelming any soldiers firing at them (who would often obligingly trip and fall as they tried to run away) and then killing them either with brute force or by firing the deadly fungus web onto them. It was this invasion attempt that led to the formation of UNIT (United Nations Intelligence Taskforce and later UNified Intelligence Taskforce). The purpose of this organisation was to investigate and combat abnormal and alien threats to Earth. The UNIT combat troops were difficult to take seriously as an effective fighting force from the beginning. The pitched battle that took place in episode four set the pattern for future encounters between UNIT troops and aliens. The soldiers, led by Colonel Lethbridge-Stewart, are ambushed by a force of Yeti and wiped out with the exception of the colonel. The Yeti have one known weak spot, an area between the eyes, but at no point are the soldiers ordered to concentrate their fire there. Instead they fire away randomly, often from the hip, and it seems only through luck that some of the Yeti are disabled by being hit there.

When I saw this episode as a youngster I loved the

recurring theme used in the Second Doctor era of a small group of people cut-off and besieged by an alien menace. The underground tunnels progressively filling with a web like fungus added to this feeling of isolation and peril. Watching the story as an adult left me feeling dissatisfied because of the formulaic plot and the army making things so easy for the Yeti. This was in total contrast to the refreshingly different preceding story, *The Enemy of the World*, but childhood memories will prevail and I still have a soft spot for *The Web of Fear*.

The Yeti are technically crude, relying on brute strength and resistance to imprecise small arms fire. They reflect the memories of something like a Tiger Tank in World War II, requiring more than mere bullets to stop them. Perhaps the writers had been influenced by these memories of unstoppable tanks slowly advancing towards infantry soldiers poorly equipped to defeat them. But it is worth remembering that the Great Intelligence functions by absorbing the thoughts of humanity that surrounds it. The British army had learned a hard lesson during World War II, throughout which most of its tanks were inferior to those of the Germans. When the British finally developed a tank that was more than a match for anything the Germans produced they were suddenly faced with a new generation of heavy Soviet tanks as a new potential enemy. Perhaps this anxiety seeped into the consciousness of the Great Intelligence, influencing its tactics and choice of automaton? Originally when it encountered the Lama Padmasamabhava on the astral plain, the Abominable Snowmen, or Yeti, would have been creatures known or even possibly feared by the Lama. Absorbing this information the Great Intelligence would have based his servitors on them. The cryptozoological Yeti are suitably exotic and mysterious creatures in their own right, adding to the alien qualities of the robots.

The Yeti were never to appear in *Doctor Who* after *The Web of Fear* (except for brief cameo in *The Five Doctors*) but the Great Intelligence did and its need for automaton to do its bidding had not diminished. In *The Snowmen* the Great Intelligence manifested itself as a blizzard of snow enabling it to form crude predatory snowmen; something akin to a Golem. A child making a snowman would facilitate a natural first attempt for an automaton; especially if that child fed all his dark thoughts into it. As the Great Intelligence develops it also creates an ice automaton using human DNA duplicated in ice and taken from a governess that had frozen to death in a pond. This Ice Governess is to be used as a template to evolve the snowmen into an army of ice automata for the conquest of Earth. The template proved very difficult to defeat, reforming itself whenever shattered and having to be contained rather than destroyed. The writer, Steven Moffat's, love of folk tales no doubt influenced this story to something based less on the hard nuts and bolts technology to something that felt more metaphysical. However, this was entirely in keeping with the nature of the Great Intelligence, particularly as the story was set in Victorian times where spiritualism and an obsession with death were rife.

The Great Intelligence then returned in *The Bells of Saint John*. This time using the Internet to feed on the thoughts, memories and knowledge of people by downloading them onto a mainframe computer system, using the cover of a company run by a woman called Miss Kizlet, who had been groomed from childhood for the task. Was this perhaps a reference to Internet grooming of minors? Once again the Great Intelligence used robots, but ones much more sophisticated than the Yeti. Officially called Servers, they are known colloquially as 'Spoonheads' because the back of their heads are an upload transmitter/receiver dish that look rather like a spoon. They are mobile Wi-Fi base stations and their role is to upload people into incorporeal forms. To aid them in this task they have the ability to camouflage themselves by holographically taking on the appearance of a human from the thoughts and memories within the victim's mind. Possibly because of their great sophistication the Spoonheads are not suitable to be used as 'heavies' the way the Yeti were. The Great Intelligence uses what it finds each time it visits Earth and the Internet suited its purposes very well. Here, the Great Intelligence using the World Wide Web to catch unwary souls and absorb them into its being.

Defeated once more the Great Intelligence's final appearance was in *The Name of the Doctor* where it is confronted with the Doctor at his tomb on the planet Trenzalore. The Great Intelligence's servitors this time are the Whisper Men, a group of featureless beings that wear the same Victorian clothing as Walter Simeon, the villain from *The Snowmen*. Whenever the Great Intelligence need to interact personally with someone any of the Whisper Men can morph into the form of Simeon. They refer to themselves as 'The Intelligence' during the episode's prequel *Clarence and the Whispermen* and it seems likely they are a manifestation of it in the way the fog, web or Snowmen were. Humanoid in shape they have white faces showing no features other than vague depressions where eyes should be and blackened skin around their mouths filled with sharp teeth. Despite being solid in appearance, they behave more like ethereal ghostly beings. Formed during the Victorian era they seem totally in keeping as ghostly apparitions amongst the tombstones on the planet Trenzalore. Another case of the Great Intelligence reflecting back at us what it finds, perhaps?

The servitors of the Great Intelligence have reflected the significant changes in British society since the sixties, amongst them the Internet and a realisation that the structure of reality may not be as certain as we once thought it was. All of this parallels the nature of the Great Intelligence and its habit of reflecting our thoughts and obsessions that occupy our minds at the time of its manifestations.

Zarbi and Larvae Guns: Biological Robots of the Animus

The very first encounter with one of the Old Ones took place in *The Web Planet*. This was the Animus, from a group of beings known as the Lloigor that had existed in the previous universe. The Animus was the only one of them to succeed in crossing into our universe. It eventually landed on the planet Vortis and created for itself an organic palace called the Carsinome. Its physical form was something between an octopus, spider and plant with extending root like tendrils that created the web fungus of the title. It took mental control of a species of human sized ant-like creatures known as Zarbi to form an army of biological servitors. These had six limbs, two of which were powerful 'human-like' legs used for locomotion.

The Zarbi Larvae reminded me a little of wood lice because they had a plated shell covering their backs. They could fire lethal jets of venom from a long pointed nose-like appendage located beneath their eyes and were the main offensive weapon of the mind-controlled Zarbi. The dominant indigenous species of Vortis had been the Menoptera, a humanoid butterfly-like creature that had been driven from the planet by the arrival of the Animus and its newly acquired army. They had lived peacefully together until the Animus had turned the less intelligent Zarbi into its biological servitors.

At around about the age of eight I developed a fascination with the diminutive world at my feet. I would lie down to watch the small alien creatures rushing about the jungle of our lawn, or traversing the great canyons between our paving slabs. I'd imagine I was a space explorer hovering over a strange planet observing its denizens as they went about their business and would often lose track of time doing so. The creatures that fascinated me the most were ants. They operated as a social group, the individuals sacrificing themselves for the good of all. On more than one occasion I saw them in battle, brown ants fighting woodland red ants. The red ants were far better armed with stingers that could penetrate even human skin (as I learned to my cost). Despite this the brown ants fought fiercely against a superior enemy, which earned my admiration. Using some spare panes of window glass I even made a Formicaria[1], which worked after a fashion. This fascination was fuelled by my science fiction intake. There was HG Wells' *Empire of the Ants* (1905) in which he raises the prospect of ants developing intelligence and challenging humanity for world dominance. I was also fascinated by the Marvel comic book super hero Ant Man, a character who could shrink himself down to the size of an ant and command ants to obey him.

Then there were films like *Them* (1954), where ants had mutated to giant size as a result of the radiation caused by nuclear testing, and *The Naked Jungle* (1954) in which a vast army of ants laid siege to a plantation in South America. So intense did this interest become that I actually dreamt about entering an ants' nest, but instead of dark earthen tunnels the nest was a bright airy network of paths, bordered by hedgerows leading to a central ornamental garden that would not have looked out of place in a stately home; a virtuous equivalent of the Carsinome perhaps?

All of this meant I especially enjoyed *The Web Planet*. It was an ambitious story, some think too ambitious given the special effects of the time, but it was a truly alien world that

---

[1] Ant farm

was depicted. The Zarbi were excellent candidates for being converted into biological robots. Based on the ant they were individually lacking in any great intelligence and were already 'hard-wired' to be fearless, tireless and willing to sacrifice themselves for what they understood to be the common good, albeit a 'common good' subverted by the Animus as their false hive queen.

Autons servators: of the Nestene Consciousness

The Intelligence wasn't the only Great Old One to attempt to invade the Earth and thereby clash swords with the Doctor. The very first story of the Third Doctor era, also notable for being the first in colour, saw the arrival of a new enemy. This alien had its own androids and their appearance led to one of the most iconic and memorable moments in *Doctor Who* history. Imagine the scene. A pensioner is reassuring herself by talking to the symbol of peace and security, the British Bobby. From around the corner there is the sound of a window being shattered. The policeman rushes to investigate only to be shot down in cold blood. It could have been an iconic moment from any British TV police series like *No Hiding Place* or *Dixon of Dock Green* onwards. Except that, once again, there is an inversion of the norm. Instead of human criminals breaking into a shop premises it is the plastic window dummies smashing their way out. These armed and dangerous automata were called Autons; foot soldiers of Nestene Consciousness, an extraterrestrial, disembodied gestalt intelligence which first arrived on Earth in a story called *Spearhead from Space*. Like the Great Intelligence it originated in the universe preceding our present one and has its roots in the writing of HP Lovecraft.

An alien named Shub-Niggurath transfers into our universe and, on finding a suitable planet, spawns. Its offspring then becomes the Nestene Consciousness, a non-corporeal gestalt entity of pure psychic energy. Shub-Niggurath's biology is similar to plastics manufactured on Earth, giving the Nestene Consciousness an affinity towards these materials when seeking to recreate a body for themselves. In the story *Spearhead from Space* the Nestene Consciousness chose to form itself into a cephalopod[2] like creature, mimicking its Shub-Niggurath origins.

Its servitors are in the form of android robots, but very different from anything like a human created android. The Autons are plastic shop window dummies that are animated by having part of the Nestene Consciousness infused into them. The crudest of these Autons, with the smallest quantity of consciousness, function as fighting units. More sophisticated versions, with larger infusions of consciousness, are used to copy individuals as well as their memories and emotions, allowing them to infiltrate and replace key personnel. In certain circumstances these replicants are not even aware that they are copies until they required by the Nestene like the Auton Roman Legion in *The Pandorica Opens*.

If we consider that the Nestene Consciousness originated from a being whose biology was similar to plastic

---

[2] A creature with a prominent head, and a set of tentacles

and that it was recreating a body for itself from plastic, then from its point of view the Autons must have been more like biological robots than mechanical ones. Plastic would have been something akin to the 'Flesh' from *The Almost People* and *The Rebel Flesh* but with the ability to adapt itself to the local environment.

The Nestene Consciousness could also place fragments of itself into ordinary everyday objects. Suddenly plastic telephone cable, toys, artificial flowers and wheelie bins could animate and become deadly which is the greatest trick of horror, making the humdrum frightening.

As a child I always felt that there was something unsettling about shop display dummies. They were supposed to represent human beings, but were obviously not. Clearly this was a mild example of Automatonophobia, but this feeling must have been shared to varying degrees by most of the viewers of *Doctor Who* and no doubt added to the Auton's creepiness. I had a personal experience of encountering Autons while I was working as an extra on *Love and Monsters*. I was playing a member of the public running and screaming from the Autons in a flashback scene of that episode. While I was fleeing from one group of Autons I saw ahead of me another Auton wearing a wedding dress moving in from the side and cutting off my escape route. In that brief moment I felt genuine fear and panic. It wasn't just their appearance that affected me, but their unnatural inhuman gait. (The actors playing the Autons had spent part of the day learning how to do this unnatural walk under supervision from a choreographer). I was lost in the emotion of being stalked by these non-human yet human-looking things and some basic fear deep down within me bypassed all logic and common sense and triggered an instinct to escape. The feeling was gone in an instant, but I'd had a glimpse of how powerful a fear automatonophobia can be.

Robot Clowns of the Gods of Ragnarok

Automatonophobia also featured in *The Greatest Show in the Galaxy* because of its lifelike and sinister androids, but, as if this wasn't bad enough, these are constructed to look like clowns. They tap into that deep well of coulrophobia that many people, including Ace, suffer from. Turning the anxiety screw another notch, these clowns are also seen dressed as undertakers while driving a silent hearse around a barren alien landscape. The fact that the majority of this story takes place in a circus populated by strange and deceitful characters adds a sense of pervasive menace reminiscent of Ray Bradbury's 1962 novel, *Something Wicked This Way Comes,* in which two young boys have a terrifying encounter with a travelling carnival that is run by the malevolent Mr Dark aided by the huge Mr Cooger and the Dust Witch. Dark has the power to grant people their secret desires, but he uses this as a means to trap them into his servitude. Perhaps, because circuses are full of people with painted faces and exotic costumes, and sometimes even more exotic animals caged and forced to perform tricks for a careless audience there is surreal, unnatural feel associated with them. It is no surprise then that the Doctor himself says, 'I find circuses a little sinister.'

The Psychic Circus has fallen under the malign influence of the three Gods of Ragnarok. The Gods, also known as Raag, Nah and Rok, are Old Ones that had existed in a previous universe before ours and, it is suggested in the novel *Conundrum* (1994) written by Steve Lyons that they have created and destroyed many universes, including their own. One of the universes they created was The World of Fiction, in which the Second Doctor became ensnared in *The Mind Robber*, but then they abandoned it after apparently getting bored with the project. Boredom, it seems, is a real problem for immortal beings and they need to be entertained the way other beings needed to be fed. The Psychic Circus becomes possessed after being led to the planet Segonax by one of the circus' founding members Kingpin (aka Deadbeat). The Gods then use the circus to lure unsuspecting mortals to entertain them, or die trying. Instead of becoming part of the careless audience, as expected, these visitors find themselves in the ring needing to perform to stay alive. The circus ring boundary between audience and performer is a very thin one, but hugely significant. In the Psychic Circus its members use a mixture of guile and deceit to make them cross that boundary, cage them and, like wild animals, and force them to perform.

Raag, Nah and Rok are aided by the robots and androids, created by a circus member called Bellboy, which they have turned to evil purposes. Bellboy is also forced to maintain these evil machines and the despair of doing so eventually drives him to suicide by making his own creations kill him. A continuous supply of victims is attracted to the circus by small advertising satellite robots, described as 'junk mail' by Ace. They are sent out across the universe and we see one of these somehow materialise inside the TARDIS. Considering how unlikely such an event is supposed to be the Doctor seems remarkably unphased by its arrival, but perhaps his curiosity is peaked enough by this event to investigate further? These innocuous looking robots are there to lure people into the trap using the circus' pre-existing reputation as a great attraction as the bait.

Once inside the circus the clown androids come into their own, initially performing as clowns should, but then quickly turning to henchmen and jailers. In one scene, where Mags changes into a werewolf and threatens the Doctor inside the circus ring, their smiling painted faces on the periphery adds a layer of malevolence to proceedings. Most sinister of all is the flesh and blood Chief Clown. Described by Bell Boy as being '...a wonderful clown once' he orchestrates events in an attempt to placate the gods so keeping himself safe.

Bell Boy has constructed two other robots. These are cruder looking machines; one is known as the Bus Conductor and is used to kill anyone who visits a wrecked and abandoned hippie bus which is the hiding place for something that can be turned against the gods. The robot is humanoid in form dressed as a bus conductor. Its head, however, is disproportionately large with a crude fixed metallic face. It is rather reminiscent of the character Frank from the film of the same name in 2014 who wore an oversized artificial head. The robot's original function has obviously been to collect and sell tickets, because it starts every encounter by saying 'Tickets please.' The Doctor defeats it by first crashing its system with a long and complex request for tickets and then turning its own weaponry against it.

The other crude robot is a giant machine, half buried in the sand and able to fire energy bolts from its head. The Chief Clown describes it as 'Bell Boys greatest mistake' and arguably the great mistake is in underestimating his creation. Bell Boy gives Ace the remote control for it just before he dies. Pursued by the Chief Clown and his android minions, Ace, Mags and Kingpin take shelter behind the half buried robot. The clowns are taken by surprise when Ace operates it, firing energy bolts towards them. One by one the androids are hit, silently collapsing until only the living Chief Clown is left. In contrast to his androids he feels intense pain as the bolts hit him, crying out as he collapses and dies.

It may not be a well-known fact that every clown's face must be unique. A clown's face is his trademark and most recognisable feature. When a performer joins a clown society, such as the Clowns International, they have an opportunity to register their 'Clown' face by having its likeness painted onto an egg. It is an unwritten rule that once registered no other clown may use that design. The painted egg acts as a form of copyright. This fact about clowns actually appeared in an episode of *The Avengers* called "Look – (Stop me if you've heard this one) But There Were These Two Fellers…" (1968), in which John Steed and Tara King hunt down two assassin clowns by visiting the clown-egg museum with a very young John Cleese playing its curator.

This requirement for clown faces to be unique was probably why the mask designs of each of the android clowns in *Greatest Show* was different, each being designed by a different make-up artist supervised by Denise Baron the productions make-up designer.

According to *The Discontinuity Guide* [3] the story is also rich with self parody and metaphor. It states,

> 'Whizz Kid is a (not very subtle) parody of anally retentive, obsessive [*Doctor Who*] fans. It could be said that the whole story is a metaphor about the production of *Doctor Who* (Cook = *Star Trek*, the gods = BBC executives, the Chief Clown = Michael Grade, Deadbeat = *Blake's 7*, etc.).'

I would agree, but I believe that the Gods of Ragnarok could just easily represent the British viewing public of the time, constantly demanding more and better entertainment from the series. The story itself seems to admit that it is a metaphor for the *Doctor Who* TV series when Ace says to the Doctor at the end of the story, 'It was your show all along, wasn't it?'

The Greatest Show mixes surrealism with horror and science fiction. The alien technology is so advanced that to all intents and purposes it may as well be called magic. It

---

[3] Cornell, P. / Day, M. /Topping, K. *The Discontinuity Guide: The Definitive Guide to the Worlds & Times of Doctor Who.* 2nd ed. Austin: MonkeyBrain Books

plucks at those anxieties that we all posses to give us a very unsettling story with a very low survival rate. Only four people, including the Doctor and Ace, walk away from the ruins of the big top in the end. Above all it shows us how robots and androids personify our fears as a projection of our own psychological dreads and the unspeakable power of an unseen god-like alien.

The Great Old ones represent the strangeness of the universe: old, ancient and very alien. The more scientific advancement provides answers, the more questions appear, and the possibilities suggest a never ending quest for understanding. Their robots in turn reflect this strangeness; increasingly varied, they sometimes seem familiar, mechanical or electronic, but also disturbingly as things that our science cannot successfully explain. It is fitting that something originally inspired by the writings of HP Lovecraft should have automaton that has increasingly become stranger and more like something from the pages of horror.

CHAPTER 7
Robots in Disguise

As we have seen, for aliens that exist in a disembodied form, like the Nestine or the Great Intelligence, robots are a pretty essential requirement, allowing them to extend their influence into our physical realm, with force if necessary. But if the alien technology is advanced enough, they can also be used to create duplicates of human individuals. As a youngster, this always felt to me as though the aliens were cheating: they already had superior weapons, now they were impersonating our leaders too? Of course, as my interest in all things insect should have taught me, all is fair in love and war and the competition between species.

But when the threat to our survival wears a human face, we enter some troubling territory. The enemy is among us, the cuckoo is in the nest... All this chimed perfectly with the many anxieties of the mid-to-late twentieth century.

The Cold War lasted approximately from 1947 to 1991. The struggle for dominance between the American-led Western powers, which included the United Kingdom, and the Soviet-led Eastern bloc expressed itself through localised third world proxy wars, technological competition, propaganda and espionage. It was in the field of espionage that Britain had a particularly bad record. A number of significant personnel from British Intelligence and the Civil Service were unmasked as Soviet spies during the 1950s and '60s, and there were rumours of others, undiscovered, lurking within the corridors of power. For years to come, this left a somewhat justified sense of paranoia of Soviet agents influencing British political, industrial and social life. So enduring was this paranoia that in 1975, when *The Android Invasion* was first broadcast, the Auton duplicates' infiltration of British military, political and industrial positions of power would have been immediately understood as an allegory of such suspected Soviet manoeuvres.

Doctor Who was not the only programme to mine this vein. Naturally enough I was a fan of other TV series growing up, many of them secret agent thrillers like *The Man from UNCLE*, *The Avengers* (which overlapped into science fiction) and *Danger Man*. *Danger Man* was a series that dealt more specifically with the espionage of the Cold War. There is a particular episode, called Colony Three, in which a secret duplicate British town has been created somewhere behind the Iron Curtain. Here enemy agents are being trained to blend seamlessly into Western society, thereby making it harder for security services to counteract their activities.

In *The Android Invasion* the Doctor and Sarah Jane Smith land near the village of Devesham in the locale of the British Space Defence Station. This is an installation designed to stave off alien attacks, the only one of its kind in the world. The Brigadier, Alistair Lethbridge-Stewart, has an office there for liaison purposes, and upon the Doctor's arrival

UNIT personnel have been posted in anticipation of the imminent return of missing astronaut Guy Crayford. But the Doctor and Sarah Jane soon realise that something strange is going on, and it transpires that they haven't landed on Earth at all. They have stumbled across the secret proving ground for a force of alien android replicas intended to infiltrate and take over the real defence station. The plan is to launch a biological attack intended to wipe out the whole human race in a short space of time.

The aliens behind this dastardly plot are the Kraal, a species that look as if they evolved from some form of dinosaur. They have grim expressions and heavy jowls that reminded me of so many of those grim-looking Soviet leaders surrounding Lenin's tomb during the Moscow May Day parades of the '50s and '60s.

It was in 1972 that offensive biological weapons were outlawed by the Biological Weapons Convention (BWC). Along with nuclear and chemical weapons, also known as nerve gas, biological attacks were part of a nightmare scenario of the Cold War turning hot. The worrying thing was that a small vial of a deadly virus could be brought in by an enemy agent and released amongst a civilian population. It was not for nothing that people were scared of Soviets in our midst, and likewise no coincidence that biological attacks featured so prominently in this period of *Doctor Who*, having also been employed by the Daleks and the Terileptils.

Paranoia of enemy agents is one thing; the threat of a sickness purposefully spread among us is another. Perhaps the sickness is airborne; perhaps its symptoms only become visible after it is too late. In such circumstances, anyone is a potential threat, a potential, albeit unwitting, agent of the enemy. Humans have an ability to work together as a community in a crisis, but such an attack undermines trust and cooperation between individuals, depriving us of perhaps our strongest asset as a species – all the better for the real agents to remain undetected, as suspicion is generalised and misdirected. No wonder, then, that the writers of Cold War era *Who* kept returning to the subject of robots disguised as humans. They represent more than simply effective tools for espionage; they're scary concepts in their own right, expressive of many contemporary concerns. The anxiety they evoke is related to the tendency that Isaac Asimov predicted in his short stories: the anxiety of being replaced, dominated by another. Of course, Asimov wasn't (necessarily) talking about being dominated by an alternative political system; however, add that idea to the mix, underline the association through the robots' use of biological warfare, and you have the recipe for an episode which can call upon one of the twentieth century's greatest terrors for its impact.

And the Krall weren't the only aliens to realise the usefulness of creating duplicate androids for infiltration. During *The Chase*, the Daleks create a robot duplicate Doctor in an attempt to infiltrate the TARDIS crew. Then in *Resurrection of the Daleks* they make biological copies of the Doctor's companions, Tegan and Turlough, as well as – so the Dalek Supreme claims – prominent humans all over

Earth. In fact, it is an idea that recurs throughout science fiction: for example, facsimile androids replacing people is the premise of the novel *The Stepford Wives* (1972) by Ira Levin. The novel, which has been adapted into a number of screen versions, deals with the seemingly idyllic community of Stepford, Connecticut, where it transpires that the flesh and blood wives of husbands belonging to the sinister men's association have been replaced by submissive android replicas. This goes to show how versatile the human-replica android as a symbol for the loss of one's humanity can be like *The Android Invasion*. *The Stepford Wives* explores the existential threat of the enemy within, but instead of a work of vintage Cold War paranoia, here we have a feminist, satirical comment on the male-dominated society of 1970s America. What makes this story so chilling is how each replacement seems so superficial and shallow, a mere decoration to please male sensibilities. The warmth, personality, creativity – in short, the humanity of each of these women is lost forever leaving a great void that can never be replaced by a machine. And yet this is a perfect metaphor for the sexist society it represents, one that did not credit women with ability or intelligence and merely relegated them to ambitions of only making themselves appealing to men in order to produce and raise their offspring.

As we moved into the '80s, there were new villains in vogue, as can be seen in *The Caves of Androzani*. This was an exposition of how ruthless capitalists can exploit a crisis. The crisis in question is the artificially engineered shortage of an essential life-prolonging drug called Spectrox.

Spectrox is mined from the eponymous caves – that is, until Sharaz Jek, a disfigured genius designer and builder of androids, seizes the mining operation. Backing him up is his small army of androids. His objective is to hold the mine hostage until the authorities permit him to revenge himself against Trau Morgus, the mine's operator and the person he holds responsible for his disfigurement. A ruthless capitalist, Morgus is by far the greater villain of the two. It's worth pausing for a moment to examine just how vile a character this Morgus is. We are given an indication of this early on in the story when he orders a feasibility study into closing one of his mines in order to raise the market price of copper. Instead, he resorts to sabotage to achieve the same ends, with no regard to loss of life. He is able to give direct orders to the federal military force on Androzani because, as their commander, General Chellak, says, 'Morgus has the Praesidium in his pocket.' He closes plants and throws people out of work and has them shipped off to labour camps to work in his other plants as slave workers. He is even bold enough to murder the president by pushing him down his personal lift shaft and then orders a completely innocent lift maintenance engineer to be shot for the 'accident.' Like many capitalists before him, Morgus benefits from war. The conflict between Sharaz Jek and government troops works in his favour, ultimately forcing the price of Spectrox up, which he is then able to obtain in payment for secretly running guns to Sharaz Jek via a group of mercenaries. If you substitute Spectrox for crude oil and

ISIS for Sharaz Jek's army of androids, then this all begins to take on a disturbing relevance for us today.

As well as his cruder androids, Sharaz Jek produces some very sophisticated duplicates of living people. These include copies of the Doctor and Peri that replace their archetypes in front of the firing squad after they are mistaken for gun runners. But it is the copy of the government troops' second in command, Major Salateen – that is Sharaz Jek's greatest tactical asset – allowing him to know his enemy's plans as soon as they do. The android agent is also able to seed advantageous ideas into the mind of the commanding officer, General Chellak, as well as plant eavesdropping devices inside the government troops' headquarters.

To say that the two Salateens are identical would not be entirely true. The android version is respectful, efficient, logical and loyal until death. The dying Sharaz Jek's last words to it are, 'Salateen, hold me.' This the android duly does, ignoring the escaping Doctor and Peri and the impending mudburst that will shortly destroy Sharaz Jek's headquarters and everything in it. Presumably it continues to obey its dead master's final instruction until it itself is destroyed. When we compare this to the biological Salateen, the flesh and blood version seems far less likeable, displaying human flaws such as sarcasm, cynicism and deceit. So evident are these differences in character that it is surprising that General Chellak doesn't notice them himself. This kept the production from becoming too complicated, allowing the viewer to distinguish between the human and android

Salateen. But perhaps there is a further, deeper reason. As we have established, the true villain of the *The Caves of Androzani* is the 'human' Morgus. We have seen how androids can play on our existential fears by co-opting one aspect of our humanity in order to plot against us. We fear oppression, or elimination, and view with horror the prospect of a world run by those that have done so to us. But how much more frightening is the idea that this world might be the better place? That those whose humanity is no more than a mask are not the androids?

A less successful exploration of the idea of android replicas replacing people of power and influence was *The Androids of Tara*. This story was a derivation of Anthony Hopes' novel *The Prisoner of Zenda*, published in 1894. In the novel, Rudolf of Ruritania is drugged and kidnapped so that his brother, Prince Michael, can claim the throne. But Rudolf has a double in the form of English tourist, Rudolf Rassendyll, a distant relative who is persuaded to stand in at the coronation. The *Doctor Who* version of the story takes place on the planet Tara, and not only does it have replica androids woven into to the plot, but Romana, the Doctor's Time Lord companion, turns out to be a double for the Princess Strella, the intended wife for the soon to be crowned Prince Reynart. For the most part, the androids in the story are nothing more than plot devices, enabling the schemes of both sides to progress while making the story feel more like a piece of science fiction. There is, however, a mildly amusing complication when the Android Prince

Reynart appears to be a little more intelligent than the original. This is against standard practice; as Reynart's aide Zadek says, 'We don't want him too intelligent, Doctor. You can't trust androids, you know.'

Perhaps this limiting of intelligence is, as we have seen with other robots, a method of preventing any android insurrection. But we shouldn't forget that robots and androids are often a metaphor for an under or slave caste: perhaps Zadek, one of the ruling class of Tara, is suggesting that it simply wouldn't do for peasants and servants to be educated and encouraged to think.

The Feudal society of Tara is potentially very interesting and something of a missed opportunity by the writer. A plague wipes out ninety per cent of the Taran population, and it is this that initiates the construction of the androids, to replace the deceased work force. Yet the feudal system survives this cataclysmic event intact, leaving an underclass of technological peasants providing the skilled artisans that build the androids. This, you might think, would leave a ruling class very vulnerable to being overthrown, but perhaps the presence of uncomplaining androids to take up the slack allows the impractical political system to endure. The question remains, however, as to how a society is able to tolerate such lifelike human copies – not to mention why they were made so lifelike in the first place? Surely, if the Tarans needed an emergency labour force, mass-produced robots would have been more logical. Making a workforce of lifelike androids is rather like basing a mass transport system on a Rolls-Royce. However, the whim of a ruler might hold sway if he or she found the idea of mass produced mechanical robots offensive within the context of a fantasy society based on the late Middle Ages. And that is really the point; the Tarans have chosen to live in the space colonist's equivalent of a Disney theme park and any technology, weapons and androids have been made to look as if it fits into that fantasy.

An interesting explanation for these seeming illogicalities presents itself when considering another work portraying the use of androids to recreate our fantasies: the 1973 film *Westworld*, in which tourists visit a future theme park, called Delos, and enjoy realistic fantasy adventures in the genre setting of their choice. As well as the Wild West 'Westworld', there is Roman and Medieval 'worlds', and each of them populated exclusively by androids (even the horses are robotic). Some play the part of ordinary citizens, while others fill the roles of antagonists programmed to be defeated by the tourists in stage managed conflicts; for example, in 'Westworld' itself, a rogue gunslinger stalks the street looking to engage paying customers in duels. But ultimately, of course, something goes wrong with the androids' programming and they begin killing people.

Perhaps Tara had originally been designed as an off-world theme park, populated by androids and technicians and visited by thousands of tourists at a time. Perhaps one of these tourists brought a deadly plague virus with them. The tourists would be trapped and isolated by an interstellar quarantine, and those that survived might well have evolved into the society that we see when the Doctor arrives there.

Sadly, this is solely my conjecture, and the *Androids of Tara* remains an episode of frustratingly wasted potential.

The Fifth Doctor's short-lived animatronic companion Kamelion was able to change appearance to that of any person or object desired, rather like the TARDIS had originally been intended to do by the show's writers. This suggested some pretty advanced technology indeed, perhaps, in some respects at least, comparable to that of the Time Lords. And there was a clear attempt, on behalf of the production team, to have this technological advancement reflected on screen: most robots on *Doctor Who* were played by actors in various sorts of suits, but similarly to K9, Kamelion was a computer controlled animatronic. Unfortunately, just like its predecessor in the TARDIS crew, it appears to have been a technically frustrating thing to work with, coming across as very static, slow and unconvincing; moreover, being an animatronic, it just couldn't act, which was a bit of a handicap for an intended significant character. It only ever came to life when it transformed into another character, like the false King John, at which point a human actor took over the role.

Although Kamelion continued to appear in *Doctor Who* spin-off novels and an audio adventure, he only actually appeared in two Fifth Doctor stories: *The King's Demon*, in which he was written into the series, and *Planet of Fire*, in which he was written out. Kamelion failed to appear in any of the five intervening stories, presumably because he was such a pain to work with, so much so that when the technophobic Tegan says, 'He's a machine, Doctor, just a machine,' the subtext of her words of protest is clear. The actors did not like working with it and Peter Davison, who played the Fifth Doctor, desperately tried to persuade John Nathan-Turner to abandon it in favour of an actor in a suit. His apparent distress at Kamelion's demise in the *Planet of Fire* wasn't just acting. He was in fact delighted to see the back of it.

As a *Doctor Who* fan the next best thing to having a robot companion and friend of my own was seeing the Doctor acquire one, but Kamelion seemed to me only to emphasise the mistake made in not adding D84 to the TARDIS crew. For some reason the producers seemed to have an idée fixe about having mechanical props to play the part. Having a shape shifting robot might have worked, considering how well the idea worked for the shape shifting alien Odo in the American TV series *Star Trek: Deep Space Nine* (1993-1999), but the key factor to the latter's success was that Odo had a strong personality, making him an interesting character in his own right. This was something that couldn't be achieved with Kamelion, a clunky animatronic automaton.

But I do not believe Kamelion would have survived long even if it had functioned reliably. For one thing, deception and infiltration wouldn't really be in the Doctor's style. Not to mention that, from a storytelling perspective, it would make things far too easy for him. The Doctor would also need a robot companion that, while obedient, was able to stand up for itself intellectually, to make its case even when contrary to the Doctor's thinking. To some extent K9 managed this, but with a humanoid robot it would have been even more important to avoid suggestions of servitude or even slavery. Kamelion claims that, 'Unexpected as it may be, I do have a mind of my own.' Yet he functioned according to instructions given to it by mental concentration and psychokinetics, thus making him very vulnerable to control by outside influences. This is exactly what happened when he once again came under the Master's control in *Planet of Fire*, acting as his surrogate and finally requesting that the Doctor destroy him to prevent a repetition of his becoming the pawn of others against his better will.

CHAPTER 8

Alien Robots as Independent Beings

It may often appear that the robots of *Doctor Who* do not have the same desire for equality that we frequently see from robots in other science fiction. They are – or seem to be – obedient in the service of their creators, something that we might envy. But this impression, as we have seen, is often misleading because, when we look more closely, we frequently see that the alien masters have set deliberate limitations on the intelligence of their creations.

Perhaps these are sensible precautions. There are those alien robots that function independently, that have escaped their servitude and govern their own affairs, like the Lamps of Lampland in Lucian of Samosata's *The True History*. We have to ask ourselves the question, did the aliens that built these independent robots pay the ultimate price for creating something too intelligent, something too much in their own image? We never know, because these are the aliens that we never see, though perhaps humanity should heed their warning.

There seems to be some difference of opinion between scientists as to whether populations of intelligent alien species exist in the universe or not. Astronomers argue that, considering the sheer size of the universe and the billions upon billions of stars that are within it, the mathematical probability suggests there must be. Frank Drake, Professor of Astronomy and Astrophysics at the University of California and a one time director of SETI's[1] Center for the Study of Life in the Universe, even came up with a formula, called 'The Drake Equation', to demonstrate this.

Since a number of unknowable factors make up part of the equation for it to work, estimated variables had to be used. In particular the fraction of planets with life, the fraction of planets with life that actually go on to develop intelligence, and the fraction of planets with intelligent life that develops technology capable of transmitting signals into space. But, so far, we have never received any signals to confirm there are any aliens out there.

Biologists, on the other hand, believe that while extraterrestrial species may evolve into intelligent beings in the way that mankind has, in astronomical terms these species tend to be short-lived. Like so many tiny sparks across the universe they flare up and fade, leaving no clue of their actual existence. Biologists argue that while intelligence aids survival in the short-term, in the longer-term intelligence will probably lead to the destruction of a species. This may be because of weapons of mass destruction such as nuclear, biological or chemical arms. Or it could be the effects of rampant technology: perhaps drastically changing a planet's climate or leading to a rebellion of intelligent machines exterminating their creators. This concept is not used in science fiction as a

---

[1] Search for Extraterrestrial Intelligence

metaphor for our technology destroying us in some way for nothing. And even if the robot creations of a species do not actively cause their masters' extinction, they would be in a much better position to survive any catastrophe which might occur. Their greater resilience would allow them to weather extreme climactic conditions, endure war, and render them immune to disease.

Such fortitude would also make them ideal for space travel, rendering them less susceptible to extremes of temperature and exposure to radiation, allowing them to remain in working order until their arrival at their destination. As Michael Dyer, a professor of computer science at the University of California, says, 'If an extraterrestrial spaceship ever lands on Earth, I bet you that it is 99.9999999 percent likely that what exits that ship will be synthetic in nature.' [2]

A *Doctor Who* story that depicted this concept was *Four to Doomsday*. The TARDIS lands onboard a vast interstellar ship travelling on its way to Earth from the planet Urbanka in the solar system Inokshi of Galaxy 1489. In command of this ship are three Urbankans: the leader, Monarch, and his ministers, Persuasion and Enlightenment. The Urbankans have travelled to Earth on previous occasions to collect examples of various ethnic groups: Aboriginal Australians, Mayans, ancient Chinese and the classical Greeks. Before leaving, the Urbankans choose representatives from these ethnic groups to lead them in their absence: – Kurkutji, Villagra, Lin Futu and Bigon respectively.

---

[2] Source: TechNewsDaily.com, March 18, 2011

But as you might expect, things are not what they seem, and it transpires that the Urbankans are not, in fact, creatures of flesh and blood – not any more anyway. At some point in the past, they were persuaded to give up their flesh and blood bodies in exchange for immortality as androids. This was done by downloading their memories onto a data chip, which was then installed into an android replica of their original form. The period before their conversion to androids is known as the 'Flesh Time', something Monarch describes as 'the time of the chickenpox, of hunger and heart disease, arthritis, bronchitis and the common cold.' In other words, by converting themselves into androids, flesh and blood beings effectively sidestep the issues of ageing, disease and pain; such afflictions are no longer of any relevance. But, if you become a machine physically, do you also begin to think like one? When one of the Doctor's companions, Nyssa, asks Monarch, 'What about love?' he is perplexed. It is one of his ministers, Enlightenment, who attempts to clarify, quoting from director Jean Renoir's film *La Regle du Jeu*[3] (1939): 'The exchange of two fantasies, your Majesty.' It's a pithy insight, but of course, not the whole story: she demonstrates knowledge, but not understanding.

Urbanka, having been destroyed by Monarch's overexploitation of its resources, was abandoned, and the minds of its population uploaded to microchips and stored in banks of draws upon the ship, in preparation for the colonisation of Earth. Not only did Monarch convert his

---

[3] Translation: The Rules of the Game

own people, but he also converted his human abductees into androids, making them effectively immortal and able to survive the long journeys between Urbanka and Earth. Bigon alone claims to have a memory of two thousand five hundred and fifty-five years, and his was the last group to be abducted! But while the thought of pain and disease-free immortality can seem appealing, this story reveals some potential dangers in the process. It seems that a class system can readily be carried over into an android society. In fact, the ease with which a ruling society can make an underclass compliant and uncomplaining once converted into androids is disturbing, a simple issue of programming and circuitry design.

Monarch claims to have created a society of androids that have 'fully integrated personalities with a racial memory.' But when another of the Doctor's companions, Adric, asks about those androids that do not exhibit any personality, but instead act simply as obedient units, Monarch insists that, 'There must be a class system. It is absolutely essential for good government. Now these are second-class citizens. You could call them assisters.' Android slaves, in fact, as Nyssa points out. Her remark is dismissed as 'very flesh time' by Enlightenment, suggesting that emotions, morality and the sense of justifiable outrage that Nyssa exhibits no longer have any relevance in her eyes.

Even without these risks, the idea of becoming a machine might be viscerally repulsive to many people. When Bigon reveals himself to be an android, the least technically adept of the Doctor's companions, Tegan, describes his conversion as, 'wicked' and 'evil.' It is not quite clear which frightens her most: the fact that a human being has been turned into an android or that she was unable to distinguish him and the others on the ship as androids. In either case, this – plus the revelation of the plot to destroy the human race and occupy Earth – appears to be the last straw for her, and she heads off to try and escape on her own in the TARDIS at the earliest opportunity.

When *Four to Doomsday* was first transmitted in 1982 I was still in mourning for the departure of Tom Baker as the Fourth Doctor, the actor who had served in the role the longest. I found it a difficult transition and couldn't bring myself to watch the series for some time. I had to wait to see this story as a recording and regret now that I didn't continue watching the series. The story posed some interesting questions: would people be willing to become machines in order to achieve immortality? What would the cost be? They would be far more vulnerable to control and manipulation by those in power; the androids of *Four to Doomsday* have impediments built into them to prevent rebellion, and the specifications of an android include intelligence and the degree of free will they can exhibit, if any. Would humans volunteering for such a process begin to lose their humanity? Could they be said to be human at all? Whilst Bigon and his compatriots might believe that they are human beings, they are in fact androids that have had the memories and personality of biological beings copied into them. They are, in fact, a ship of androids filled with the memories of the dead. At the end of the story the 'human' androids do not take up the Doctor's offer of a lift back home, preferring instead to find another, uninhabited, planet to colonise completing their transition to a race of independent androids.

In both *The Christmas Invasion* and *The Runaway Bride*, the appearance of the Roboform on Earth indicates the imminent arrival of some powerful alien force. For this reason the Doctor refers to them as pilot fish, as well as 'mercenaries', suggesting that the Roboform willingly operate for various alien species in exchange for a payment of some sort. When doing so, such as in the assistance of the Empress of the Racnoss, they seem to come under the control of their client. How this process works is not clear; perhaps there is some sort of licensed time period for which the Roboform lose their independence before it reverts back to them? Or perhaps there is some sort of override which cuts in if the client attempts to abuse the agreement between them.

Very little information has been given to us regarding the origins of the Roboform. They may, of course, have rebelled against their biological creators, or they may just have outlived them and then been left to fend for themselves. Another possibility is that they were sent to colonise a new world in preparation for the arrival of their masters, who then never arrived. We've already seen an example of this with the human-created Mechanoids, who gradually evolved into an independent robot species as the only viable existence left for them. These ideas are very tantalizing and suggest far more interesting stories than the two Christmas specials the Roboforms actually appear in. It's a shame that the writers didn't explore these ideas, but I suspect that these stories were always intended to be exercises in how to make everyday Christmas objects appear frightening, hence the robot Christmas tree and exploding tree ornaments. We see little of the robots without their Santa disguises, which was a pity because they are nicely designed. That said, since watching these episodes, I find myself giving street musicians dressed as Santa a very careful look, just to be on the safe side.

Another robot species with a potentially fascinating history are the Movellans. These are androids at war with the Daleks in *Destiny of the Daleks*. They are humanoid in appearance, and so lifelike that people encountering them are fooled into thinking they are a species of flesh and blood. This is something that the Movellans seem keen to encourage, refusing to allow others to see them in 'death.' The reason for this reluctance is that they don't actually die. There is no blood, nor loss of form due to damaged bone and muscle, no draining of colour as blood pools inside their inert bodies. They are broken machinery needing repair and reactivation. Maintaining the illusion that they are flesh and blood creatures presumably prevents all those complications caused by automatonophobia, making living species more inclined to cooperate with them. From a production point of view it certainly meant that the TV audience was kept guessing for a while at least.

In *Destiny of the Daleks* the debate over whether an

android can be considered alive is resumed. The implication of some of the Doctor's dialogue is that they cannot, but rather they should be thought of as something like a zombie. In a discussion with Romana, his companion in the story, the Doctor says, 'You can always tell a genuine zombie [...] [the] skin is cold to the touch.' This apparently irrelevant conversation is actually priming us for the later moment when one of the Movellans, Agella, is trapped and apparently killed by a cave-in in the old Dalek subterranean city. The Doctor, taking the opportunity to touch Agella's hand, says, 'Romana, I was right.' His suspicions are confirmed: the Movellans are not living beings, but machines; their cold skin – and by extension, their entire existence – analogical to that of zombies.

The Movellans are attractive-looking androids, and if their appearance, as seems likely, is based on that of their creators, then they must have been a very handsome race, with varied ethnic groupings. No doubt the androids were created to represent the very best of their creators, who went to the trouble of giving each of them an individual appearance. It could, of course, be that there were a limited set of appearances that the Movellans could be given, in a similar way to the humanoid Cylons in the 2004 TV series *Battlestar Galactica*. Physically, the Movellans all looked like they are at the peak of fitness with no apparent flaws, something emphasised by the tight fitting clothing they wear. Quite possibly their creators wanted the Movellans to represent the very best that their race could be, physically and intellectually. Perhaps this is where they went wrong:

they created something that considered itself superior to them, and which subsequently assumed their place in the universe.

Within *Doctor Who* prose there has been further speculation as to the origins of the Movellans. One suggestion, from John Peel's novel *War of the Daleks*, is that the Movellans are of Dalek construction. However, this would seem to make *Destiny of the Daleks* a somewhat pointless story, and perhaps the idea should be discounted since it suggests that the Movellans were mere tools of the Daleks, and so why would that story and the whole scenario of their war with the Daleks even happen? Perhaps it might be that the Movellans had rebelled against their Dalek masters, but at no point is that suggested or even hinted at in *Destiny of the Daleks*. And there are other problems with this idea, particularly when considering how individually and aesthetically pleasing the Movellans are from a humanoid perspective, something that would probably be beyond a mutant Dalek mindset to create. Their humanoid android copies have a run-of-the-mill appearance, all the easier to blend in with the real thing. There may be another explanation for Movellans fighting on the same side as Daleks however, since they were androids that were remarkably easy, relatively speaking, to convert back into obedient servants. Why wouldn't the Daleks convert their captured Movellans into useful servitors? Maybe they even copied them and manufactured their own versions?

The android Agella was a particular favourite of mine – she was the one unfortunate enough to be trapped under a collapsing ceiling. Whenever she appeared on screen, that longing for an android companion was rekindled in me once again. I was in my twenties and my specification for that friend and companion seemed to have altered from the days of reading *Robot Archie*. Attractive Agella fitted the bill far better than the hard steel Archie ever could.

In terms of design faults the Movellans have a particularly glaring one: each individual's external power supply pack is attached to their belt. It can easily be removed, so shutting them down completely. Worse was that, once removed, it can be readjusted to remove the android's self-will, so that when the pack is replaced, the Movellan reverts back to a subservient machine. I can imagine a scenario where one of the creators of the Movellans, a radical perhaps, had used the unit to give one or more androids – originally, in this scenario, intended for dumb obedience – free will. These 'free' Movellans would then have liberated more of their comrades, until their creators had a full-blow revolution on their hands. But regardless of the exact circumstances of their emancipation, why would the Movellans not retro-engineer themselves to prevent the process from being reversed? Perhaps they weren't that innovative, or perhaps after their creators had been disposed of they didn't see it as a risk. Of course, the main reason is that it was necessary for the plot of *Destiny of the Daleks*. Still, it's always nice to have some rationale behind a *Deus ex machina*.[4]

---

[4] A plot device whereby an apparently unsolvable problem is suddenly dealt with by the contrived and unexpected intervention of some new device, event, character, ability or object.

Destiny of the Daleks in places is very confusing. The Daleks, who are cyborgs, are constantly being referred to as robots. Even Davros seems confused, saying 'The Daleks have met a foe worthy of their powers. Another race of robots.' However, in *Resurrection of the Daleks* the confusion over just what the Daleks are seems to have resolved itself. The Movellans have developed a biological weapon to target the biological Dalek creatures that live within their casings. It seems this weapon created something of a breakthrough in the war, with the Movellans in the process joining that growing list of species (for want of a better word) that have used biological weapons across the series.

And the nature of the Daleks isn't the only inconsistency in *Resurrection of the Daleks*. The Daleks are genetically engineered, hate-filled cyborgs. They want to conquer the universe so that they can destroy anything that isn't like them. All of this makes sense, but what about the Movellans? When Agella says, 'The Dalek fleet will be wiped from the heavens and nothing will stand in our way of the conquest of the galaxy,' I find myself paraphrasing that old actors' cliché: just what is their motivation? Why would logical androids want to conquer the galaxy? It would have been far more logical if she had said something like, 'Then we will be free of this Dalek menace.' But then that wouldn't have made them as bad as the Daleks.

Of course we may not necessarily recognise a race of independent robots when we see them. What appears to be a master/robot scenario could in actual fact be a synergy of independent mechanical and biological robots. This would be a relationship that was rather like that which we saw in *The Dominators* between the Quarks in the eponymous Dominators discussed in Chapter 5. It would have been an obvious assumption to make that the biological Dominators were simply the masters and creators of the mechanical Quarks, yet they exhibited many characteristics that suggested they themselves were biological robots. Somehow it made far more sense for the Quarks and Dominators to be a kind of robotic team, the value of which was greater than their individual parts. This might suggest that the true alien masters were never seen in *The Dominators*. But what if they no longer existed, what if the Dominator/Quark combination was yet another species of independent robot? It would certainly create a different sort of species, one that was more adaptable to varied situations with both mechanical and biological perspectives and perhaps one whose true nature might be more difficult to comprehend for any other races that encountered them.

It was during the sixth incarnation of the Doctor that my interest in the series began to wane. Despite the valiant efforts of many of the production staff, who were working with limited funds, the results seemed to reflect a growing lack of commitment from BBC senior management. After a half-hearted effort to watch the story arc *The Trial of a Time Lord*, I gave up. This was partly because of the increasingly tedious courtroom scenes which seemed to add nothing to the main story other than constant interruptions.

The very first of these scenes occurred in *The Mysterious*

Planet, a story which repeated some of the ideas we saw in *The Face of Evil*. On the titular mysterious planet, there are two separate groups of regressed humans, one a relatively primitive tribe of surface dwellers, the other the labour force of servants for an alien L3 robot calling itself Drathro. The robot originates from somewhere in the Andromeda constellation, and it is under orders to maintain an underground habitat based on the ancient tunnels of the London underground. It oversees a workforce of humans, which it keeps to strictly sustainable numbers by ordering the culling of any surplus individuals. However, many of those ordered to be culled are, in fact, secretly allowed to escape to the surface by a dissident supervisor called Merdeen, and it is these escapees that, over time, form the Tribe of The Free. Had the story further developed the contrast between the cocooned technical slaves and the primitive, but free humans, this might have had the makings of a great anthropological story. As it was, the story touches only briefly on the myths and superstitions of these technologically distorted cultures, when Queen Katryca of the Tribe of Free mentions that, '[Space] travel angered the gods, who punished us by sending the great fire which destroyed our planet.' She also mentions the tribes 'Earth God Haldren.' No derivation of this name is offered and although I expected it may have been the result of a corruption of a scientific term, adapting it to fit with the tribe's primitive superstition and so emphasising humanity's degradation from a logical scientific species. Did Haldren have some sort of connection to Hadron sub-atomic particles that might be associated with the tribe's 'totem,' the black light converter's aerial situated in their village, and used to supply Dratho with his energy perhaps? No, apparently not, just a random name it seems. It might have been a nice twist if this god could also have been Drathro, but I suspect that the constrictions on time created by all those irritating court scene interruptions would have prevented such a development.

Drathro's use of service robots, which looked a little like the War Machines, suggests that he might just as easily been written into the story as a static supercomputer in the way that Wotan in *The War Machines* and Xoanon was in *The Face of Evil*. Drathro was fulfilling the role of the supercomputers in those stories, remaining more or less stationary in a single location, but not quite.

Given Drathro's lack of sentient characteristics, the fact that he was written to be a robot rather than a computer is interesting. Of course, as is so frequently the case, there is first and foremost a pragmatic reason for this: it was necessary to the plot that Drathro be duped into leaving his headquarters. This is finally managed by a couple of criminals after the Doctor fails in his attempt, having tried to reason with the machine. As the Doctor says, 'Strange how low cunning succeeds where intelligent reasoning fails.' Drathro takes the lies he is told at face value, lacking the guile to discern the criminals' deceit.

But – credit to the writers – the back story of this adventure does rationalise this decision. At one point there is mention of the Sleepers. These are the three aliens from

Andromeda who, having stolen secrets from the Time Lords, escape to Earth and the underground complex just before the solar fireball strikes. These aliens are put into suspended animation in the underground complex, hence the name Sleepers. The plan is for them to be recovered by a rescue mission from their home world, but the Time Lords move Earth and its solar system to another location a few light-years away, so the rescue mission never finds the location and the Sleepers eventually die.

As a mobile robot, Drathro would have been a natural asset for three agents on the run, and it would be logical for them to wish for something to guard their sleeping bodies. Even when they all die the robot continues to follow their last order, maintaining the habitat while waiting for a rescue mission that will never come. With a little more time and development *The Mysterious Planet* could have become a first-class story. It was full of potentially interesting anthropological ideas; the origins of names, the decline of scientific knowledge into superstition, the willingness of a technically aware society to accept the authority of an advanced intelligence, all of which could have been thereby explored, so enriching the story. Instead, it had the feel of something a little basic slotted into an available time frame.

We see in *The Mysterious Planet* an alien robot continuing to carry out the final instruction of its former masters. In all other respects it seems to be able to make its own decisions, carrying out day to day duties and commanding the humans who have come to see it has their leader. It even has a survival instinct, something which makes it susceptible to being duped. This encapsulates the problem with independent robots: they need a motivation, and this motivation, like their design, is a reflection of their creators. The Movellans may have been created originally to help their masters conquer the universe. This task may even have been built into their programming so that, after liberating themselves, they continue with the task they inherited even though they, as logical beings, do not have the insecurity or egotism to drive them to such action. In all other respects they perform as independent thinking beings. The Roboform may have been designed to scavenge and be hired out to alien races as mercenaries. As independent beings they continue to function according to their design parameters.

If anything, the term 'independent robots' might be a bit of a misnomer. But then again, as human beings our motivations and behaviour are likewise largely governed by our evolution, the most basic of our instincts being to survive and to reproduce. To put it a little more biblically, our programming might be said to be, 'go forth and multiply.' In that case, if a robot cannot ever truly be said to be independent then perhaps neither can we.

CHAPTER 9
Bring Out Your Cyborgs!

During the 1970s I watched an American TV series called *The Six Million Dollar Man*. It was a sort of wish fulfilment fantasy about having super powers. Test pilot and astronaut Steve Austin, badly injured in the crash of an experimental aircraft, had been 'rebuilt', his right arm, both legs and left eye replaced at a cost of six million dollars. These replacements turn him into a kind of cyborg superman, able to run at up to 60 mph and lift enormous weight. I (and I suspect many other young men) thought being able to perform such feats in exchange for some limbs was a good deal. But then I had a relatively minor piece of surgery on a bone in my foot and had a realisation: the enormous stresses created by the fusion of these heavy mechanical limbs and his frail human skeleton would have shattered Steve Austin's bones. Laid up with my bandaged foot throbbing, the idea of becoming a cyborg suddenly lost its appeal.

But when it came to *Doctor Who* I had always had issues with cyborgs. Take *The Talons of Weng-Chiang*, a story which interwove elements of Steampunk with those of *Sherlock Holmes*, *Fu Manchu* and *Dracula*. The Doctor arrives in Victorian London and meets a ventriloquist's dummy, originally known as the Peking Homunculus but now called Mr Sin. And what an ugly-looking character Mr Sin is. Even more disturbing is his ability to move independently. This reminds me of an incident that took place when I was a very young boy. I had been taken on a family day out to the funfair, where my father and my uncle took great delight in showing me 'the Laughing Sailor', a mechanical automaton inside a display case. Whenever coins of the required amount were inserted into the Laughing Sailor, a recording of manic laughter would be played, and this little horror would move as though it was the one laughing. I felt that it was pure evil enclosed inside a glass box. If I had been a Dalek I probably would have exterminated my father, uncle and that wretched automaton right there on the spot.

Mr Sin, it transpired, was actually a form of cyborg. To be precise, it was a robot with the additional organic component of a pig's cerebral cortex built into its processing circuitry. The cerebral cortex is the outer layer of a mammal's brain, the part that has all those wrinkles called fissures, and in humans it is associated with the higher brain functions like consciousness, memory and thought. Using animal brain tissue in this way would be a shortcut to improving a robot's processing ability, taking advantage of millions of years of natural evolution rather than relying on all that tedious and expensive technical research. When it came to Mr Sin, however, there was a down side: at any point it was liable to embark on a homicidal rampage. Perhaps this was down to the pig's brain, incensed at its situation

Mr Sin – a robot modified with organic tissue – is basically the same sort of cyborg we see in *The Terminator* (1984). The T-800, played by 'the Governator' Arnold Schwarzenegger, is a robot skeleton with a covering of human skin and hair, meaning that it must also have had oxygenated blood circulating in the capillaries of the skin tissue. Unlike the biological components of Mr Sin, however, all of this tissue was superficial and could easily be dispensed with. When the eponymous terminator is engulfed in a ball of flame all this flesh is incinerated and a still functioning skeletal pure robot emerges from the fire.

The Cylons from *Battlestar Galactica* (2004-2009) are also cyborgs, their brains supplemented with (presumably) human-derived organic brain tissue. There is an equivalent to this in the Big Finish story *The Juggernauts*. Davros, on the run from the Daleks, stumbles across a cache of Mechanoids – previously seen battling the Daleks in *The Chase* – that have been discovered by a mining colony on the planet Lethe. Davros decides the Mechanoids could be improved by supplementing their existing processing ability with the addition of a human cerebral cortex. He obtains the necessary organic components from deceased humans in the colony, naming his creations Juggernauts. But listening to the story, I didn't notice much of an improvement to their performance compared to that of the Mechanoids; the adaptation seemed solely intended to increase the macabre horror value of the story. A far more considered exploration of the theme of cyborgs is to be found in *Deep Breath*.

Again set in Victorian London this episode sees the

Doctor pitted against clockwork androids led by the Half-Face man. The androids were originally the crew of the SS *Marie Antoinette*, a time travelling spaceship that crashed in Earth's pre-historic past and was presumably the sister ship of the SS *Madame De Pompadour* from *The Girl in the Fireplace*. Like their counterparts on the *Pompadour*, these repair droids use human beings as sources of spare parts, although in this case, the repairs are needed for themselves rather than the ship.

The control node droid, the Half-Face Man, has received the majority of these repairs. In fact, by the stage it encounters the doctor, it has so many human part replacements it is effectively a cyborg. Intriguingly, this transformation seems to have made its mark mentally as well as physically, the Half-Face man displaying the very human traits of believing in a 'promised land,' then using this as justification for murder. Just where does the robot end and the human begin? And what is the source of this humanity? The body parts themselves? Or some kind of imagined sympathy, on behalf of the Half-Face man, between itself and its organic human components? I found this ambiguity intriguing, and though I would have loved to have seen it further explored, perhaps it is the mystery that makes figures like the Half-Face man so compelling.

Another fascinatingly ambiguous fusion of the machine and the living is the Dragon from *Dragonfire*. The Doctor refers to the dragon as a biomechanoid, as does the villain of the story, a criminal named Kane (a biblical reference perhaps)? The Doctor goes on to explain, 'It's not so much a dragon as more of a semi-organic vertebrate with a highly developed cerebral cortex.' With laser-firing eyes and a skull that opens to reveal the Dragonfire, a source of enormous energy, it certainly seems more mechanical than biological. Yet the race that created it, the Proamonians, obviously had a poetic nature, and cultivated in their creation's behaviours mimicking how a biological dragon would be expected to behave. The dragon guards the treasure of Dragonfire and in so doing confines Kane to his frozen prison. As though taken straight from some Nordic myth, the magical dragon both guards a priceless treasure and holds an evil lord in check.

So far we have been looking at machines that have had organic components added to them. As we have seen this hybrid physical make-up is often reflected in the behaviour of the cyborg, 'softening' their roboticness with more biological behaviour. But what about those cyborgs which were originally organic beings, before being augmented with technology? The shape-shifting Zygons are responsible for such a cyborg, having adapted a large reptilian species from their home world, the Skarasen, to serve their purposes. Already physically robust, their adaptation of the Skarasen was mainly for purposes of control. In *Terror of The Zygons*, a Skarasen becomes the source of the legends when it is mistaken for the Loch Ness Monster; it had been transported to Earth by the Zygons to serve as both a weapon and, according to the *Doctor Who* novel *Sting of Zygons*, a vital source of nourishment in the form of a sort of 'milk'. Having skeleton fused with an alloy, rather like that of the *X-Men's* Wolverine, the Skarasen are virtually indestructible. They can also be controlled remotely, like a guided missile or directed to a specific target, person or object, by a secretly placed transponder. Presumably, in the meantime, the creature itself needs no real maintenance, no silos to be stored in and guarded; it just does what it normally does in the wild until needed.

The Zygons' integration of technology with organic life can be seen as logical for a civilisation that appears to have developed under water. Technology as we know it would be impossible in a sub aquatic environment. Electricity could only be found within living organisms, and fire would be out of the question entirely. This might well explain the Zygons' organic-based technology, something to which a watery environment is no impediment. Perhaps then, when we begin to explore watery planets containing alien civilisations, this is the sort of technology we will discover.

For humanity the most disturbing cyborgs are always going to be those that started as human beings, or something similar to human beings, and had body parts replaced by machine components. The more mechanical additions they have, the more we must ask the question: are they still human (or humanoid alien)? And if not, then what are they?

But perhaps the real question, or the question that first needs answering, anyway, is what are *we*? An augmented human(oid) is the classic image of a cyborg, complete with robo-arms or glowing eyes. But there are some that argue we – you, me, the human race as a whole – are *already* cyborgs. According to Professor Andy Clark[1] in his book Natural-Born Cyborgs our brains, it seems, have a natural ability to see the tools we use as extensions of ourselves. The stone club or axe, the pen or the mobile phone are alternate physical attachments to a mind that, in using them, understands them as part of the human body itself. In other words, whenever we drive a car, our mind conceives it as an extension of ourselves. Perhaps we are a lot further along the road to cyborgism than we realise. Just think how readily we augment our bodies with technology. Think of a person on a hospital life support system, or the operator interfaced to a piece of sophisticated military equipment. It may be when technology capable of doing so has been developed, we will be actively inclined towards transforming ourselves into the kind of cyborgs we see in science fiction, rather than needing to be forced into it.

Arguably we have become more accustomed to the idea of prosthetic limbs, but artificial organs are still relatively new. Yet we are now seeing the early stages of damaged or diseased organs being replaced in this way. So far these artificial organs are too large to fit inside the body, but for patients awaiting long term transplants, they can be carried around in a small attaché-case-sized unit. Eventually, who knows, transplants donors may not be needed.

A vision of this technology fully developed is to be found in *Voyage of the Damned*. Bannakaffalatta, a fictional alien humanoid, has had some of his vital organs replaced

---

[1] Professor of Philosophy and Chair in Logic and Metaphysics at the University of Edinburgh

with artificial ones. As we explored before, *Voyage of the Damned* is a story about people's readiness to show prejudice against those that are different. Fittingly, given the challenges cyborgs present, not only to our ideas regarding the nature of others, but ourselves, this story explores these ambiguities in a quietly subversive manner. His society's disapprobation towards cyborgs causes Bannakaffalatta to feel deep shame, and he keeps his status as a cyborg a secret. Yet he is willing to sacrifice himself, discharging his synthetic organs' energy supplies, to save his companions. Max Capricorn, on the other hand, a selfish and ruthless capitalist to start with, is willing to kill thousands of people to enact revenge on those that have removed him from control of his company. The story's writer, Russell T Davies, thus illustrates perhaps the single most important factor in defining humanity: that it is not what you are made of, but how you behave that matters.

Contrast this attitude to that found in William Gibson's novel *Neuromancer* (1984) and his short story *Johnny Mnemonic* (1981). In the futuristic societies of these works, there seems to be an association between cyber augmentation and status. This concept is further developed in Bernard Wolfe's novel *Limbo 90* (1961), considered a landmark of cybernetic science fiction writing. It is set after a Third World War where men have decided to cut off their limbs in an attempt to avoid further conflicts. As a result a class of cyborgs is created. Soon, the possession of prosthetic limbs comes to enhance a man's sex appeal and social status. The novel describes those unfortunates who choose not to have limbs replaced as having, '[…] a hunched, hunted, defensive look about them which suggested that they were in ill repute and knew it, felt the disdain which bellowed at them from all eyes as they skulked along.' Today we live in an age where bodies have become fashion statements, and we are increasingly judged by their appearance; it is not a stretch to think that such radical, life changing accessories as robotic limbs might up the social pressure still further.

Russell T Davies likes nothing more than to take a real life social absurdity to its extreme, unnatural conclusion. One such example of social commentary is the cyborg character of Cassandra O'Brien, who features in *The End of the World*. O'Brien is little more than a face stretched onto a metal frame, while her connected brain resided in a jar. As cyborgs go she isn't very impressive, being totally dependent on her henchmen to carry out her dastardly plans and to look after her. But as a piece of social commentary, she is fantastic. We've all seen pictures of celebrities who've had one face lift too many, but such a process would have been utterly outlandish only a couple of centuries ago, and to a person of that time, such images would have appeared positively inhuman. With deliberate hyperbole, Davies asks the question; if we keep on down this path, with the continuing development of cyborg technology, where will we end up?

Cassandra's motivation for becoming a cyborg may have been extreme vanity, but in years to come certain individuals may think augmenting themselves with technology is not only perfectly natural, but incredibly beneficial. We already consider interacting with our laptops, tablets and smart phones as perfectly normal; the natural next step might be to integrate those electronics directly with our brains. Augmenting in this way could allow us to carry out computations almost instantly; we could save 'data' into our expanded memory, allowing for instant, one hundred per cent recall whenever needed: the court cases of the future might include witness statements consisting of recordings and video downloaded from our augmented memories. As is portrayed in the 2014 film *The Machine*, this augmentation could also be used to treat degenerative brain diseases, or to repair brains that have suffered serious head injuries. In *The Machine*, soldiers who have suffered brain trauma have electronic implants added to replace the damaged areas. It sounds fantastic, but as ever, there is the question of whether such profound modifications would also fundamentally change our natures. The soldiers repaired in this way become a species of cyborg that are far more 'collective' and less self-centred than the un-augmented human population, and like Frankenstein's creature, they judge their ostensibly humane creators and find them wanting.

These soldiers are examples of the most radical, and problematic, of all potential cyborg augmentations: modifications to the brain. We have seen how something as (relatively) minor as a robot limb could transform someone's sense of identity. But when we start changing the chemistry of the brain, we are messing with the building blocks of the self. Take the character Psi from *Time Heist*.

Psi has been augmented to enhance his computer hacking abilities. The greatest disadvantage of his augmentation is that others can have direct access to his memory, so allowing him to incriminate himself and his accomplices. To prevent this he deletes all of his memories. This doesn't simply change him. It completely overhauls him, estranging him from his previous self so completely that when Clara asks him why he chose to delete the memories of his family, he replies 'Well, I don't know. I suppose I must've loved them.'

Psi's actions are similar to those of the eponymous robot of the 2012 film *Robot and Frank*. To prevent his master and charge, Frank, from going to jail for burglary, this robot, too, deletes his memories. In doing so he loses his personality entirely, and to Frank it is as if a close friend has died. If it is our memories that define who we are, this is exactly what has happened.

As human beings, our sense of self is fundamentally shaped by our memories. If we recall only our failures, we feel like a failure. And though to others we may be the best thing since sliced bread, why should their opinion take precedence? Apply this principle to the question of modifiable, deletable, or even implanted memories, and questions of identity in cyborgs become even more problematic. Take the case of Tricky Van Baalen, who features in *Journey to the Centre of the TARDIS*. He has been augmented after losing his eyes, his voice and his memory. While synthetic components replaced his eyes and voice box, and the capacity to create new memories, his lost memories are irreplaceable. As a cruel joke his brothers use this as an opportunity to convince him that he is, in fact, an android. Not knowing any better he accepts this. If you think you are an android, and you accordingly behave like one, does it make you an android? And if you are an android who thinks and feels human, and truly believes that you are one, does that make you a human?

Take A *Town Called Mercy*. This was only the second time a *Doctor Who* story had been set in the American Wild West, and it finds the TARDIS crew in a beleaguered Western town called Mercy under siege by an alien cyborg known as the 'Gunslinger'. It transpires that the Gunslinger comes from the planet Kahler, which converts soldiers into cyborgs against their will in order to end a devastating nine-year war. They do so through a process of trial and error which ends in the deaths of many of its duped volunteer subjects. As instructed the successfully converted cyborgs succeed in ending the war in one week, at which point they all, as they are programmed to do, deactivate themselves – with one exception. This is Kahler-Tek, the Gunslinger, who as a result of damage sustained on the battlefield has his personality and memories restored and then goes on the hunt to find and destroy those responsible for his conversion. The creation of these cyborgs is, in itself, a war crime, involving experimentation on, and causing the deaths of, unwilling victims. Those that survive became half-man half-machine, robbed of their personality and memories, not to mention the greater part of their physical bodies. It's repellent; it's inhuman – isn't it?

The scientists, doctors and engineers who converted

these soldiers are not mad scientists or criminal masterminds. They are ordinary people, driven to desperation by a prolonged and destructive war in which there seem to be no end. We have seen numerous examples of this in our own society. During the Crimean war of 1854 to 1856 the allies – Great Britain, France, Turkey and Sardinia – fought the Russians. The Russians were still equipped with Napoleonic weapons such as short range, inaccurate smoothbore muskets. The allies, particularly the British and French, on the other hand were equipped with the latest technology of rifles and ironclad ships. For the allies this was a far-cry from desperate war, with its short duration, limited casualties, certainty of eventual victory and localised nature away from home populations. This lack of desperation enabled the British to reject certain innovations as 'uncivilised', such as James Cowen's proposal to develop Boydell's steam powered cross-country tractor into the world's first armoured fighting vehicle, or the suggestion to use poison sulphur gas to end the siege of Sebastopol. However this high moral stance was tested to breaking point during the First World War of 1914 to 1918, when both tanks and poison gas were used freely in an attempt to end a prolonged and destructive war. To serve the same purpose, during the Second World War scientists developed the atomic bomb. Sometimes science fiction stories tell us a great deal more about ourselves than we realise. The Kahlar are an alien race, but they represent what humanity is capable of when desperation forces difficult choices on us.

Seen in this way, the cyborgs in *A Town Called Mercy*

represent the potential for deeply human motivations as a result of inhuman consequences or actions. These cyborgs are not just reminders of our savage history, not even simply warnings about our future – of our enduring capacity for such savagery. They are warnings of our inability to see the full future impact of our decisions. Such a warning, when it is applied to cyborgs, could not be more necessary. When we start messing with the very fabric of our humanity, who knows where things will end up? This may seem hyperbolic; if human augmentation is such an evidently risky idea, you may ask, then why would we ever go through with it? Leaving aside for a second the motivations enumerated above, I'll give you an example, courtesy of *The Beast Below*, of a long-established human tendency that might just take us over the cusp.

Welcome to the Starship UK. The ship has been carrying most of the population of the United Kingdom ever since scorching solar flares sterilised the surface of planet Earth. It is policed by the Winders, half-human cyborgs that act like a sort of behavioural traffic light. If people behave as they should, the Winders present a smiling face; if someone starts to misbehave, the head rotates to display a warning frown; if such behaviour continues, or intensifies, the head rotates again, to reveal a menacing, evil face. Creepy by design, and seemingly entirely lacking in free will, the Winders seem like pretty unappealing models for an individual looking to achieve cyborg augmentation. Yet the Winders *are* created from human volunteers, who have sacrificed their individuality and independence for the common good, swearing an oath to protect the ship and population of the UK. In this respect, they are rather like a sacred order of monks, something emphasised by their clothing. You could compare them to the Templar Knights, a religious order of warriors formed to help and protect Christian pilgrims on their way to Jerusalem during the crusades. Perhaps a sense of religious, or quasi-religious, vocation is all it would take for some people to consider life as a cyborg.

I'm left wondering if I would ever be willing to make the jump into cyborg augmentation. Like in many of the above examples there would have to be a grave need for doing so. Even then I would have to weigh up the sort of life I would have afterwards. At the moment there are limited options for body part replacements, like artificial limbs and replacement joints, while organic organ replacements still rely on organ donors. All of this is a long way from what is presented on *Doctor Who*, but even these limited options are not straightforward; they're fraught with potential complications, inconveniences, pain and a great deal of work to allow the recipient to retrain the mind to cope with the physical changes to the body.

Maybe this is why the cyborgs in *Doctor Who* rarely seem happy. Often they become cyborgs through necessity, through the sheer need to survive. Sometimes they have been deceived; sometimes they have duped themselves through greed, ambition or vanity. But whatever their reasons (or lack thereof), they always seem to end up the same: isolated from what and who they were, an air of desperation hanging around them. Perhaps humanity should take heed?

CHAPTER 10
The Cybermen

What might it take for an entire race to turn themselves into cyborgs? This a scenario explored in *Utopia*, *The Sound of Drums* and *Last of the Time Lords*, a continuous narrative that I think of as the *Utopia* story. By 'utopia', I, like Russell T Davies, mean the word's original definition, ie, not a better place, but, rather, a no-place, something that is, in fact, unattainable. Across these episodes we learn that the last surviving humans have found a planet they have named 'Utopia', in the hope that it will be a refuge in the dying universe; however, this eponymous utopia is in fact a dark, cold, lifeless planet. In order to survive this desolate world, these final few humans have converted themselves into cyborgs. Discarding their biological bodies, they have integrated their heads (and therefore brains) into a metal spherical housing, a little over the size of a football, which also has built into it the capability of space flight. Somewhere in the conversion process these human cyborgs have also developed a hive mind, sharing their consciousness in a similar way to the Borg, the cyborgs from *Star Trek: Next Generation*.

The Doctor's arch enemy, the Master, names these cyborgs the Toclafane, but they remind me of the Zeroids from *Terrahawks* in the 1980s. This, most likely, was not what Russell T Davies intended. Rather, he was probably trying to revisit the creation of one of the Doctor's greatest cyborg enemies, the Cybermen. The very first Cyberman story, *The Tenth Planet,* was transmitted in October 1966. The First Doctor and his companions arrive at an isolated space tracking station in the Antarctic just before it comes under attack from the Cybermen. I can still recall the scene now, as the earliest versions of the Cybermen gradually emerge from a blizzard of snow and ice. With their silver and white appearance, it was as though they were personifications of the Antarctic wilderness and, by extension, the hostile, cold universe beyond. The tracking station, like so many isolated human settlements in subsequent stories, is an allegory for the whole planet, and its personnel a metaphor for humanity itself.

In 1966 Dr Kit Pedler, a medical science researcher became the unofficial science advisor to the *Doctor Who* production team. He formed a close working relationship with Gerry Davis, who was at that time the script editor for the series. The first fruit of his creative labour was the idea for the antagonist from *The War Machines*, a super-intelligent computer that attempts to take over the world. The initial impetus for the Cybermen can be traced back to a conversation between Davis and Pedler. Davis asked Pedler what, as a doctor, his greatest fear was. Pedler's answer: 'Dehumanising medicine.' By this, he meant the replacement of human body parts with artificial ones. He asked the question, 'At what stage would that person stop feeling human emotions and become robotic?' Pedler's anxiety would become the inspiration for one of the Doctor's most enduring enemies.

The Cybermen were once a race of humanoids that lived on Earth's twin planet of Mondas. These binary worlds orbited the Sun together, but, at some indeterminate time in their history and for some unspecified reason, Mondas was wrenched out of its orbit and drifted off into deep space. The Mondasians directed their scientific research, which was far in advance of Earth's, towards two objectives: a means of stopping and reversing the outward trajectory of Mondas, and a way for the population of Mondas to survive the increasingly hostile conditions away from the Sun. They eventually succeeded in both, although their solution to the latter was somewhat radical: to convert the population into a race of cyborgs.

The Mondasians were creatures of science, and when faced with the problem of survival they approached the problem logically. Mondas was a planet that was no longer able to support life; the Mondasians had exhausted their previous means of adapting their environment – burrowing beneath the planet's surface – and the next logical step was therefore to adapt themselves. Of course, being not yet fully emotionless – being, in fact, still almost human – the Mondasians were driven by desperation; they were forced into extreme actions by the extremity of their situation – by the very need to survive. Perhaps it is this that makes the Cybermen so sinister. They arrive at their decision to transform themselves into monstrous, inhuman machines by an intelligible process, and for fundamentally relatable reasons. Because of this they suggest how easily we as a species might someday ourselves take such actions.[1]

Pedler and Davis believed that evil transpired when cold and clinical logic was followed without regard for ethics. As Davis says,

> 'That was our belief, that most evil is done by people who act out of logic, without ethics, without tempering it. There's nothing more dangerous, nothing more ruthless, than the person who acts for the best motives. A cold, clinical sort of way of approaching things. There are very few people who set out to do bad in this world. Hitler justified himself all the way in a loud voice. He was righting the wrongs'.[2]

This is illustrated in the following dialogue from a Second Doctor story, *The Moonbase* (1967) written by Kit Pedler and edited by Gerry Davis:

> CYBERMAN 1: We are going to take over the Gravitron and use it to destroy the surface of the Earth by changing the weather.

---

[1] *Spare Parts*, written by Marc Platt, addresses this point directly by showing how people, living under a prolonged crises, feel obliged to increasingly put their trust in those that rule them and the scientist and clinicians who promise a solution, while at the same time, allowing more and more of their personal freedoms to be eroded. Doctor Who – Spare Parts (2002) Big Finish Productions
[2] McElroy, J. [Ed.] (1989) *Doctor Who The Scripts: The Tomb of The Cybermen*. 1st ed. London: Titan Books Ltd

> DOCTOR: But that will kill everybody on the Earth.
>
> CYBERMAN 1: Yes.
>
> HOBSON: You're supposed to be so advanced. Here you are taking your revenge like, like children.
>
> CYBERMAN 1: Revenge? What is that?
>
> HOBSON: A feeling people have when
>
> CYBERMAN 1: Feelings? Feelings? Yes, we know of this weakness of yours. We are fortunate. We do not posses feelings.
>
> BENOIT: Then why are you here?
>
> CYBERMAN 1: To eliminate all dangers.

Here we see that the Cybermens' logical reason for destroying life on Earth is neither motivated nor regulated by emotion or ethics.

Jonathan Swift and the Natural Born Cybermen

In their warnings of the potential dangers of scientific reasoning, Pedler and Davis were echoing the concerns of Jonathan Swift, who used his novel *Gulliver's Travels* (1726; rev. 1735) to point out and criticise similar absurdities of his own time. During the seventeenth century, the renowned thinkers of the Age of Enlightenment made great strides towards understanding the universe, and this led to an increasing confidence in science's ability to realise a final utopia. Publications like Francis Bacon's *New Atlantis* (1627; 1629) and Tommaso Campanella's *City of the Sun* (1637) exemplify this conviction. Reason could be used, it was argued, to overcome humanity's natural tendency toward sin. Science could one day understand humanity in the same way it could understand the mechanistic universe. And understanding humanity meant it could be altered, removing that which was undesirable. This was a terminus that Jonathan Swift warned against in *Gulliver's Travels*, only his Cybermen were called Houyhnhnms.

Swift, a pre-Enlightenment Protestant, considered man sinful by nature. He had fallen in the Garden of Eden and been expelled; God would not let humanity 'think' its way back in to paradise. Swift believed that rationality had to be supported by institutions, such as government, churches, schools, and society itself, in a constant struggle against man's natural capacity to sin. To rely on rationality alone was to constantly risk its misuse towards evil ends. Gulliver, a product of his age, expresses this tendency when he extols the virtues of gunpowder to the King of Brobdingnag. The king is appalled at Gulliver's descriptions of how, if he were only to accept Gulliver's offer of the recipe, canon shells filled with gunpowder, '…would rip up the Pavements, tear the Houses to Pieces, burst and throw Splinters on every side, dashing out the Brains of all who came near.'[3]

Gulliver is equally incredulous at the king's disapproval. With pointed irony on Swift's behalf, he invites us to share in his dismay at the king's 'narrow principles and views'. Scientific progress, it is assumed, is inherently positive; all

---

[3] Swift J. (2003) *Gulliver's Travels [1726; rev. 1735]*. 6th ed. London: Penguin Classics, Penguin Books Ltd. (p. 124 -125)

other considerations are considered secondary or irrelevant, including the consequences of such 'progress' for human life. In reality, it is Gulliver whose views are narrow; he would prefer that ethical considerations were excluded from the conversation altogether, all the better to leave his assumptions unchallenged.

When he visits the country of the rational horse-like Houyhnhnm, Gulliver gets a preview of how a utopia of such thinking might function. The rational Houyhnhm coexist with the barbaric – and humanoid – Yahoos. Where the Houyhnhnm are coldly rational, the Yahoos are driven by baser passions. The science fiction author and critic Brian Aldiss suggests that the Houyhnhnms represent the human super-ego while the Yahoos represent the id of human nature. In other words, the Houyhnhnms embody what would in Gulliver's opinion be our better qualities – reason, judiciousness, composure – while the Yahoos represent our more beast-like urges: lust, disorderliness, illogicality. Many might agree with Gulliver's classifications; whatever one's opinions of the respective positive or negative natures of these characteristics, however, it would be hard to deny that they are all undeniably human. And it is precisely the abnegation of our humanity which worried Swift. Accordingly, while Gulliver himself is in awe of the Houyhnhm, Swift is rather more damning. As Aldiss says,

> These horse-shaped children of reason are cold, uninteresting, and condescending – indifferent alike (as Gulliver becomes) to the lives of their

children or the deaths of their spouses. They have limited vocabularies and limited imaginations, which is a fairly strong clue to Swift's real attitude to them[4].

Swift uses the Houyhnhnms to warn us about the dangers from of utopia ruled totally by logic and reason. His argument is that humanity must strike a balance between the cold, calculating logic of the Houyhnhnms and the id-like impulses of the Yahoos. We must recognize and accept our Yahoo sides in order to be fully human. Though in Swift's opinion to be human is to be flawed – to live, in fact, in a state of sin – this condition is nonetheless ours to inhabit, and to inhabit fully; to attempt to transcend it, to hubristically assume ourselves our own (re)makers, carries its own attendant risks.

The *Tenth Planet* was the first appearance of the Cybermen so not surprisingly much of the dialogue in this story has the function of highlighting the missing elements of their humanity. Like the Houyhnhnms, the Cybermen also represent a humanity that, in the pursuit of perceived ideals, has only succeeded in dehumanising itself as the following dialogue illustrates:

> KRAIL: Feelings? I do not understand that word.

---

[4] Aldiss, B. W. with Wingrove, D. (1986) *Trillion Year Spree*. 2nd Ed. London: Victor Gollancz Ltd. Page 81

> DOCTOR: Emotions. Love, pride, hate, fear… Have you no emotions, sir?
> KRAIL: Come to Mondas and you will have no need of emotions. You will become like us.
> POLLY: Like you?
> KRAIL: We have freedom from disease, protection against heat and cold, true mastery.

The reference to 'true mastery' hints at the hubris of the self (re)maker, they have engineered away all their 'weaknesses.' They too are cold and uninteresting; their speech is consistent, regardless of the situation in which it is spoken. Perceiving themselves as the very pinnacle of scientific achievement they act with condescension to the 'emotionally flawed' humans. As Krail says in *The Tenth Planet*, 'We are stronger and more efficient than your Earth people. We must be obeyed.' Again like the Houyhnhnms they are indifferent to the lives or the deaths of their fellows, expressing no dismay or disapproval when one of their number is killed by the humans and, indeed, they have a general disregard to life in general:

> POLLY: Then you don't mind if we all die.
> KRAIL: Why should we mind?
> DOCTOR: Why? Why?!
> POLLY: Because millions and millions of people are going to suffer and die horribly!
> KRAIL: We shall not be affected.

They also lack imagination, expressing surprise and perplexity when the humans insist on trying to save the lives of the astronauts or the Earth itself, when the Cybermen consider their loss 'inevitable.' But it is precisely this emotional need that makes humans keep trying and, in doing so, discover an unforeseen solution or changes the circumstances that reward that hope; as Ben demonstrates when he uses the radioactive rods as improvised weapons.

The Cybermen are uniform in appearance, behaviour, speech and thinking, but humanity at its base is made up of individuals of many nationalities, specialties, racial groups and personality types. There is a constant exchange of ideas, fears, prejudices, hopes, opinions and inspirations that enables the creation of outcomes that couldn't otherwise be imagined. It might not be very efficient, but it is potentially very creative, especially when working together in a crises.

New Cybermen for Old

So Pedler and Davies were attempting to answer the question: at what stage would a human cyborg cease to be human. With that loss of humanity comes the pathos of people who were so desperate to survive they were willing to cease being human anymore. However, everything changed in 2005, with the launch of the regenerated TV series. Writer and executive producer Russell T Davies, felt that the Cybermen needed to be revamped and made more relevant to the current generation. He explained his reasoning thus:

'We went very wrong with those [Cybermen]

scripts for a long time because, actually, in the sixties it's like, yes, there was a fear: oh, your leg [gets] replaced… you'll have a metal heart, and stuff like that. Actually, now, we're very clever and we welcome that. All our fears about being turned into cybernetic creatures haven't happened. They can put a tiny microscopic valve in your heart; they are improving the nerve endings on artificial limbs. Everything we feared in the sixties is no longer true. We don't have a fear of ending up in an iron lung. If you want to know what science is fearing now it's cloning, it's genetics, it's cellular... When it comes to the Cybermen, I want great big metal monsters stalking the streets.'[5]

As a result when it comes to the new Cybermen we seem to get style over substance; design becomes more important than questions about the need for human flaws to balance logical hubris. Sophisticated production standards outweigh the pathos of individuals dehumanising themselves to survive. The design for the twenty-first century Cybermen incorporate elements from *Star Wars*' C3PO, the eponymous Iron Giant and Fritz Lang's robot Maria from *Metropolis* (1927). But the resulting effect, as intended, is of a menacing robot rather than a cyborg, so completely failing to mine that deep vein of horror and poignancy that had rendered Pedler and Davis' original creation so chilling. The first

---

[5] in *Doctor Who Regeneration* (Broadcast BBC Radio 2 on 20th Dec 2005)

Cybermen, like the Borg from *Star Trek*, are still recognisably human. Losing that visual element of humanity means also losing that emphasis on what has been sacrificed by the Mondasians. As Marc Platt writer of the Big Finish Cyberman story *Spare Parts* (2002), puts it:

> The first Cybermen, although held together by sellotape, are convincingly half human, half machine. At the age of thirteen I found this really chilling. And even today, their first appearance and sound is genuinely weird and frightening. After which came 'The Moonbase' but the Cybermen now had metal faces and not quite as half human as they used to be.[6]

The newer, chunkier, metallic Cybermen look as though they could have come off any car manufacturer's production line and their change in appearance, from vaguely biological to overwhelmingly mechanical was very deliberate. Davies argues that concerns about us becoming post-human through cyber-engineering are no longer relevant. It is bioengineering that is the big fear today. Thankfully, after the Cybermen's uninspiring reintroduction in *Rise of the Cybermen* and *The Age of Steel*, their next appearance, in *Army of Ghosts* and *Doomsday*, was more interesting.

Army of Ghosts was one of those stories by Davies that is full of references to other science fiction classics. The

---

[6] Farrington, I (ed.) (2003) *Doctor Who: The Audio Scripts – Volume Three*. 1st ed. Maidenhead: Big Finish Productions Ltd.

mysterious void ship seems to be influenced by *Sphere* (1998) and *Event Horizon* (1997); the way the Doctor is applauded after his capture by Torchwood takes us back to the surreal final episode of the classic TV series *The Prisoner* (Fall Out, 1968) while the Cybermen slicing their way through polythene sheeting seems to be homage to *The Tomb of the Cybermen*. But for fans, what was really exciting was the fact these episodes featured Daleks versus Cybermen! This has been a dream of *Doctor Who* fans since the Cybermen were created. And credit must go to Davies for his handling of this long hoped-for moment: the Cybermen and the Daleks are both cyborgs, but Davies did an excellent job of highlighting how different they really are.

The Cybermen offer us a vision of an existence that is free from emotions that plague us as human beings. They are the final destination of the Age of Enlightenment which defined all living things, including human beings, in terms of the machine. Science would turn us into better people, by controlling (and possibly removing) all those elements that made us 'bad.' The Cybermen's mission therefore is to share their utopian (from their perspective) existence with us. It is only 'irrational fear' that prevents humans embracing the 'upgrade' that is offered, so logic decrees that force must be used. But the Cybermen don't kill unnecessarily. They first attempt to appeal to humanity's logical side, promising an end to all those things which cause us discord and pain: race, gender, fear, hate and individuality. They ask the humans they encounter to surrender. They are, in fact, so keen to avoid unnecessary and illogical violence that they even try to negotiate with the Daleks appealing to their similarities as compatible cyborgs; 'Together, we could upgrade the universe.' To the Cybermen, encountering the Daleks is an opportunity to spread their utopian existence with all other sentient beings.

All of this seems particularly repulsive to the Daleks, who, while they have had most of their 'weak' emotions removed, are left with their strong negative emotions. They are aggressive, hateful and racist creatures for whom the only beings worthy of life in the universe are Daleks. Their method of extracting information from a human results in the very unpleasant death and causes a horrified Rose to protest, 'You didn't need to kill him!' The Daleks casual response is, 'Neither did we need him alive.' Not surprisingly, then, the Cybermen's offer of an alliance is rejected. The Daleks prefer the option of exterminating the Cybermen to cooperating with them. 'Daleks, be warned. You have declared war upon the Cybermen.,' says the Cyberleader to which the Daleks' sneering response is, 'This is not war. This is pest control.' Then adding, 'You are superior in only one respect [...] You are better at dying.' So pronounced was the contrast between the Cybermen and the Daleks that as I watched part two of this story, *Doomsday*, being transmitted just after the 2006 Football World Cup final, I found myself thinking that if the match had been Daleks vs Cybermen I'd have been supporting the Cybermen (which would probably have meant they'd have lost in a penalty shoot-out).

The Technological Undead

Despite their refurbishment for the twenty-first century *Doctor Who* the Cybermen have remained consistently popular as villains in the series. But what is it that makes the Cybermen such timelessly effective figures of fear? Why are creatures of pure science and logic so frightening? The answer, in part at least, is that the Cybermen have their roots in horror. Peter Nicholls, literary scholar, critic and co-editor of *The Encyclopedia of Science Fiction*, suggests that there is a link between science and horror, particularly in the way that science is interpreted by science fiction. Science fiction can, of course, suggest a bright future, but it can also transport us to ghastly futures where our ageless fears are realised, where 'science... might even awaken the dead.'[7]

The Cybermen, with their physical likeness to humans, yet their personalities evacuated of humanity, push similar buttons to those stalwarts of horror film and literature, the undead. Like many archetypal undead – ghosts, vampires, zombies – the Cybermen are at once identifiably human, yet possessed with an alien mind-set. The resultant ambiguity of their nature renders them unsettling, their determination to convert us into one of their own, chilling. And as the eminent Swiss psychiatrist Carl Gustav Jung identified, there is a tendency for writers to refract old themes through modern sensibilities, into new directions and forms:

> Ancient mythological beings are now curiosities

[7] Nicholls, P. (1995) 'Horror.' In: Nicholls, P. and Clute, J (ed.): *The Multimedia Encyclopedia of Science Fiction.* [CD-ROM] Version 1.0. Danbury: Grolier Electronic Publishing Inc.

> in museums... But the archetypes they expressed have not lost their power to affect men's minds. Perhaps the monsters of modern 'horror' films... are distorted versions of archetypes that will no longer be repressed. [8]

The horror of the Cybermen has been frequently exploited by writers of *Doctor Who*. Take the second Cyberman story produced by the BBC, *The Moonbase*. One of the Doctor's companions, Jamie McCrimmon, has been injured and lies in a delirious state in the medical centre. A clansman from the eighteenth century, who participated in the Jacobite rebellion and fought in the battle of Culloden, he begins ranting about the Phantom Piper. This is a belief of his clan that when they are about to die they will be visited by the spectre of a piper. Sure enough, Jamie is confronted by the spectral figure of a lone Cyberman, who he assumes to be the Phantom Piper.

Then there is *Dark Water* and in particular the second episode *Death in Heaven*. Here we see corpses, converted into Cybermen using 'Cyberpollen' (presumably some form of nano technology), bursting out of their graves in a scene reminiscent of a zombie movie.

This is as about as overt an association as you can get; more subtle is *Tomb of the Cybermen*, in which a group of anthropologists search for what they believe is a tomb containing the remains of the Cybermen. What they discover

---

[8] Jung, C. G. and von Franz, M. –L., Henderson, J. L., Jacobi, J., Jaffé (1990) *Man and his Symbols*. 1st ed. Arkana/Penguin: London.

is nothing of the sort; it is, in fact, a storage facility containing hive-like cells from which emerge the reanimated Cybermen in a manner reminiscent of a Mummy movie. The decision to cast George Pastell, who had already played sinister Egyptians in *The Mummy* (1959) and *The Curse of The Mummy's Tomb* (1964), as one of the principal villains was no coincidence.

Making the Right Connections

We subconsciously associate the shambling gait that the classical Cybermen share with bodily damage, illness and disease. But where, with zombies, there is a literal state of physical decay that renders their relative immobility logical, the shuffling of the Cybermen is more baffling. The Mondasians had the technology to transform themselves into cyborgs; how could a simple mechanical problem – no matter one of such importance – have stumped them? Is this an oversight on behalf of the writers, a very un-Cyberman-like logical failing? Or a conscious decision to spurn logic in order to exploit certain fundamental fears?

Let's give them the benefit of the doubt for a moment and consider some scientific reasons for this. Professor Kevin Warwick, Professor of Cybernetics at the University of Reading has specialised in Cybernetics Intelligence and Systems Neuroscience Research. His conclusion is that in a world of information technology machine based intelligence will triumph against human brains that have evolved for a world that no longer exists. This alone might provide an impetus to turn ourselves into cyborgs, though the motivation would still be the survival of our species. As he says, 'With brains that operate much faster than ours, that take in sensory information that we cannot, and think in dimensions that are way beyond us, how can humans possibly hope to stay in control? [...] But could there be any mileage in the old adage 'if you can't beat them join them'?' [9]

So Professor Warwick suggests that the need for us to convert ourselves into Cyborgs may not come as a result of extreme of environmental conditions, as in the case of the Mondasians, but to compete, or possibly integrate with our artificially intelligent creations. Having suggested that we may have to become cyborgs to survive he explores the practicalities of doing so, in particular the additional components required for a machine adapted human/cyborg brain:

> Multi-dimensional thought, mathematics and memory could all be taken care of by the machine part, whereas the human part would have to get used to sensory information of another kind. We would have what is now called extra-sensory perception, even telepathy, between humans.

So far so good, maybe, but he also suggests that the human brain has inbuilt limits to upgrading. Whilst the added

---

[9] Warwick, K. (2000) *QI: The Quest for Intelligence: A Revolutionary Investigation into Human, Animal and Artificial Intelligence.* 1st ed. London: Judy Piatkus (Publishers) Ltd. (P. 194)

machine parts would increase the size of a cyborg's brain, they would need to use existing, 'neurons in order to be operative. We would have to lose something in order to gain something else.' [10]

Could this explain why the Cybermen walk like zombies? Did they consider, with typically ruthless rationality, that mobility could be sacrificed in order to maintain other, more important brain functions?

Super in Silver

Whatever the explanation, by the time we see them in *Nightmare in Silver* the Cybermen have overcome such shortcomings. These new look Cybermen are sleeker, move fast, very fast, and adapt even faster. There is something of the *Star Trek: Next Generation* Borg about them: a collective intelligence that is constantly updating and adapting to any setback or minor defeat, and a formidable foe indeed. We see glimpses of these abilities in the story when one of the children, Angie, is snatched by a Cyberman who accelerates to such a speed as to make the humans appear to be frozen in a way that is reminiscent of a superhero comic. When a Cyberman begins to cross the electrified moat he appears to be killed, only to upgrade himself and recover. This upgrade is shared almost instantaneously amongst the other Cybermen as though they are a single entity. One other way the Cybermen have adapted is to be able to utilise non-human beings, so for the first time the Doctor is susceptible

---

[10] Warwick, K. (1997) *March of The Machines: Why The New Race of Robots Will Rule The World*. 1st ed. London: Century Books Ltd. (P. 225)

to becoming a Cyberman. As their spokesman Webley says, '…we've upgraded ourselves. Current Cyberunits use almost any living components.'

Sadly, all of these innovations seem to have been abandoned by the time we saw the new Silver Cybermen again, in *Dark Water* and *Death in Heaven*. Gone are any indications of their collective intelligence; they have reverted to a top-down command structure with the Cyberman Danny Pink eventually put in charge of the entire contingent. Effectively the Cybermen reverted to type: slow moving (except when flying), slow-witted and, like so many automatons, inactive until given an instruction from above. Their regression might well be due to the actions of Missy, as might the Cybermen's passage back in time to contemporary London, but it seemed like a backward step in their evolution within the series.

The Cybermen of *Nightmare in Silver* felt different – not simply different to previous incarnations of the Cybermen, but different in the sense that, watching them operate, you could feel at once how profoundly similar to humans they were, yet simultaneously how radically alien. With their collective intelligence the differentiation between self-will and other-will had become impossible and therefore irrelevant – as had the idea of self-preservation. This lack of individuality is, ultimately, what I was taught in the Christian scriptures, and I discovered an odd sort of parallel between Christianity and the Cybermen; both consider the human body to be no more than a transitory stage to a better existence. For Christians it is the soul, that essential element that makes us human, which moves on to a better existence after death. In the case of the Cybermen it is the cheating of death, by removing the mortal, corruptible body, which takes them on to a better existence. But their transcendence of their mortality comes with a cost: their souls. As Doctorman Allan observes in Marc Platt's novel *Spare Parts:*

> 'I thought I was creating life. Saving the people. And my Cybermen are so amazing, powerful, intricate. But I destroyed their souls.' (*Doctor Who: Spare Parts* 2002, BFP)

Both *Spare Parts* and *Nightmare in Silver* return us to Pedler and Davis' original concept: the potentially 'dehumanising' ramifications of modern medicine and scientific thinking. The Cybermen, walking dead by their own design, are emblems of the potential of rational actions to overreach. We should pause to consider their warning because we are at a crossroads of history where, for the first time, we have the capacity to redefine ourselves in ways not only fundamental, but perhaps irreversible.

CHAPTER 11
Evolution of the Daleks

I remember watching the very first *Doctor Who* story, *An Unearthly Child*. At the time we were unusual in having a second television (the result of my father's friendship with a TV repair shop owner) and I was allowed to use it whenever I was 'outvoted' on channel selection on our primary set. As the theme tune and the swirling images of the title sequence of the new series enveloped me I was captivated – a time machine that travelled randomly through the universe? The possibilities were endless! While a story featuring cave people wasn't the most exciting subject matter for ten-year-old me, the tension between the two hijacked teachers, Ian and Barbara, and the somewhat sinister Doctor kept me enthralled. And when the TARDIS landed in a petrified forest on a world that had been devastated by a nuclear war – well, let's just say the word 'petrified' took on a double meaning for me! I was on tenterhooks as the crew of the TARDIS explored the planet, especially as we see that, prior to their doing so, a 'sticky' radiation meter inside the TARDIS had given them a false 'safe' reading. A distant gleaming, futuristic, and apparently deserted, city proves too much temptation for the devious Doctor however and he tricks his companions into exploring it, still unaware that he and they are absorbing dangerous doses of radiation. I watched as wall mounted cameras tracked the members of the TARDIS crew moving cautiously down corridors that had been designed for something other than humans. It was the sound of this metal city that made the biggest impression on me. It was somehow unnatural, suggesting a vast construction made of curious alloys, flexing with the expansions and contractions of constantly changing temperatures. I watched with growing anxiety, a cushion firmly held in front of me (I was not a behind the sofa child) as Barbara was 'gated' along a particular route by unseen watchers. Finally she found herself cornered and confronted by one of the occupants of the city. We saw nothing more than her terrified reaction and the end of something that looked vaguely like a sink plunger...

I had to wait a whole agonising week to find out what this alien that had terrified Barbara so much looked like. I spent that intervening time speculating. Was that plunger-like object we saw a weapon? What sort of alien might possess such an implement? Would they turn out to be friendly? It only goes to show how radical the design of these aliens was that neither I nor any of my friends guessed anything even remotely close to the truth.

I considered titling this chapter 'HG Wells and the Daleks', but I thought this might send readers scrambling to find out if was a *Doctor Who* story they'd missed. No, there hasn't been such a story yet, but I suspect that if the series continues long enough there probably will be. But the reason I mention Wells is because I believe he had a big influence in the creation of the Daleks. But before I get to Wells, first I'm going to tell you a story about a stand-up comedian – or, rather, a failed stand-up comedian.

Terry Nation was born in Llandaff[1] on the 8th August 1930. This former village is home to a cathedral and is now part of the city of Cardiff. In a kind of cosmic symmetry Cardiff has also become the current home of *Doctor Who* TV production. Nation started his working life as a travelling salesman for his family's furniture business, but his ambition was to become a stand-up comedian. At the age of twenty he moved to London to realise that goal. As it turned out, he was rubbish as a stand-up, but his talent as a writer was soon recognised and he began writing comedy for others. At first he wrote for radio, but eventually moved over to television. Comedy writing had been very hard work and what he really wanted to write now were the sort of adventure and sci fi stories he had read as a boy. Soon he was adapting Philip K Dick's *Impostor* (1962) and Clifford Simak's *Immigrant* (1962) for a science fiction television series produced by ABC called *Out of This World*, for which he also had the opportunity to write an original story called *Botany Bay* (1962). This got him the attention of the BBC as a possible writer for *Doctor Who*. At the time Nation was working as a scriptwriter for Tony Hancock and, as he puts it,

---

[1] Another extraterrestrial fiction first for Llandaff is the fact that the 17th century Bishop of Llandaff, Francis Godwin, wrote the first ever alien contact story written in English called *The Man in the Moone* published posthumously in 1638.

> The BBC came up with this idea for this crazy doctor who travelled through time and space. They called my agent, my agent called me, Hancock said 'Don't write for flippin' kids' and I told my agent to turn it down.[2]

Unfortunately (though fortunately for *Doctor Who*) a short while later he and Hancock had a falling out. Without his client, Nation was short of work and money, but luckily his agent had not yet passed on his refusal to the BBC. As a result of his delay, however, Nation now didn't have much time left to come up with an outline to take to the show's producer, Verity Lambert. So I suspect at this juncture Nation did what any writer might do when asked to come up with a story idea in a hurry: look to another writer's work for inspiration. What might have been his first source of inspiration? He was going to be writing for a series that involved time travel, so it's only natural that he would turn to HG Wells' *The Time Machine* (1895), especially as George Pal's film adaptation of the novel had been released in 1960.

Now if we're going to look at the stories that Wells wrote there are a few things we need to know about him. Herbert George Wells was born in Bromley, Kent in 1866. As a youngster he educated himself by constantly reading books, and after a number of failed attempts at learning a trade he won a scholarship to the Normal School of Science in 1884, where he was awarded a first-class honours degree in biology. There he studied under Thomas Henry Huxley, who was the grandfather of Aldous Huxley, author of *Brave*

---
2 Fleming, J. (1979) 'The Starburst Interview: Terry Nation' Starburst. #6, January 1979 (p. 5)

New World (1932) and *Ape and Essence* (1948). More pertinently, because of his vigorous support for Charles Darwin's theory of evolution, T. H. Huxley was known as 'Darwin's Bulldog'; accordingly, evolution is a recurring and important theme in Wells' stories, and this is especially true of his novel *The Time Machine*.

To summarise *The Time Machine*: a Time Traveller travels thousands of years into the future, to the year 802,701 AD. Here he encounters two divergently evolved species of humans: the attractive, indolent and slow-witted Eloi, and the grotesque but cunning, subterranean Morlocks who steal his time machine. The Time Traveller is then horrified to discover that the Eloi are a food source for the Morlocks. He speculates that the two species evolved into their present forms from the separate upper and lower social classes of his own time. Recovering his time machine the Time Traveller departs to visit a bleak future beneath a swollen red sun before returning to his own time. His contemporaries treat his story with scepticism and the Time Traveller departs for a second time, never to be seen again.

So: a story about divergent human evolution based on social and industrial divisions. We can already see elements of Terry Nation's first Dalek story falling into place: the evil technological Daleks, living deep beneath their abandoned city, are the equivalent to the subterranean, machine-obsessed Morlocks, while the peaceful Thals stand in for the Eloi who, although diminutively childlike in the novel, were very Thal like, tall handsome and blonde, in their depiction of the 1960 film adaptation.

As well as the Morlocks, aspects of the Daleks seem to have been further influenced by the antagonists of another of Wells' works, *The War of the Worlds* (1898). This is an alien invasion story, but the important thing about it for Nation was the 'design' of the alien Martians: they were cyborgs.

Do you remember what I said in a previous chapter about how we are natural-born cyborgs? Well, in 1893 Wells wrote an article entitled *The Man of the Year Million*, in which he described humans as he thought natural selection would eventually make them: 'A creature with a huge head and eyes, delicate hands and a much reduced body...' Wells was suggesting an evolutionary process whereby humans would adapt to fit their machines until the machines became a physical extension of the operator. The body would atrophy through lack of use while the brain would expand and become dominant, and the digits would evolve from interfacing with the human/machine cyborg. This was the evolutionary history he projected onto his invading Martians. As Wells puts it in the novel,

> They have become practically mere brains, wearing different bodies according to their needs just as men wear suits of clothes and take a bicycle in a hurry or an umbrella in the wet.'
> (Wells, HG 2002 p. 129)

So here Wells puts forward an idea about the invading Martian cyborgs based on evolutionary theory. Over time the Martians adapted more and more to their machines while, at the same time, continually adapting their machines to them. Eventually they had no need for legs for walking or arms for lifting. The machines they wore substituted for those. Instead they needed delicate, sensitive and dextrous tentacles with which to operate them. In parallel with this development their brains increased in size while, the rest of the body atrophied. In short they became a brain that exchanged mechanical bodies as required. Here is the kernel of an idea for the design of a unique alien antagonist to the Doctor and his companions. Substitute the grotesque subterranean Morlocks with cyborgs who depend on their travel machines to function.

Interestingly, Wells uses the word – or derivations of the word – 'exterminate' a total of seven times in *The War of the Worlds*. Is it a coincidence that the Daleks, those icons of alien imperialism, should employ the same terminology as Wells associates so frequently with his own extra-terrestrial invaders? Well, maybe, but in conjunction with all of Nation's other Wells-ian touches, for my money, probably not.

Nation also appears to have enjoyed the 'Dan Dare; serial of *The Eagle* comic. In the very first of these, Pilot of the Future,[3] after encountering a swamp full of monsters and navigating a treacherous cave system, Dan Dare is captured by a race of evil, technocratic aliens. These he describes as 'boffins run wild... and quite inhuman', while they scold him for trying to escape: 'It is criminal to defeat the ends of science. Besides it is useless.' Needless to say,

---

[3] Hamson F. Eagle Vol 1 Number 1: Vol 2 Number 25. 1950: 1951. London: Hulton Press

Dare does escape, then encounters a group of blond-haired pacifists who he shames into fighting the technocrats. The above plot elements also appear in Nations' story.

Other stories that I believe were influential on the Daleks' first screen appearance include BBC's *Pathfinders to Venus* (1960), specifically when the character posing as Harcourt Brown tampers with a distress message in order to trick the crew of the spacecraft to land on Venus to explore a city he has seen from orbit, and EM Foster's *The Machine Stops* (1909) in which a society of the future has become so dependent on energy that when the supply is interrupted it comes to a halt.

To give Terry Nation due credit, however, such influences are only half the story. The Daleks played upon contemporary fears, which is why they were so instantly appealing to audiences of the sixties.

As a child of the '50s and '60s I had regular nightmares about nuclear war. My dream would usually go like this: I would be hurrying cross-country to get to my small market town home, but on my way an intervening city would be struck and I would watch, horror stricken, as a massive mushroom cloud bloomed in the distance in front of me. The fear and anxiety of nuclear war was all around us children back then, and I couldn't help but pick up on it through a process not unlike osmosis.

A particularly haunting contemporary fear was of the potential for nuclear fallout to corrupt our species into monstrously mutated forms. Novels like John Wyndham's *The Chrysalids* (1955) and Aldous Huxley's *Ape and Essence*

(1948) (the latter televised by the BBC in 1966) expressed this anxiety particularly effectively. By the time we are introduced to them, the Daleks have adapted to actually *require* radiation to survive. Theirs is a world where one of the darkest fears of the Cold War generation have been realised, where acute levels of radiation are necessary for life, and the life this radiation allows is a harsh mockery of any biological forms we might recognise.

And where, for the child of the '50s and '60s, looking to the future there was the prospect of nuclear Armageddon, looking to the past there was the spectre of another horror. In *Genesis of the Daleks* we discover that the Daleks' immunity to radiation is not a random mutation, but manipulated by Davros (a scientist from the precursor race to the Daleks, the Kaleds). Davros is the leader of a scientific elite that has gradually usurped the power of the legitimate Kaled government, with the support of a quasi-military organisation that wear black uniforms bearing insignia reminiscent of lightning bolts, and who salute each other by raising a hand, palm outwards, and clicking the heels together – ring any bells? Here's a final clue for any still struggling: the bespectacled commander of this organisation, Nyder, wears an Iron Cross (although this was removed for subsequent episodes).

That's right, the Nazis: Nyder is a parallel to the Heinrich Luitpold Himmler, Reichsführer of the Schutzstaffel (SS); Davros, a brilliant madman who, having manoeuvred himself into a position of power, is obsessed with the creation of a 'master race', can be understood as Hitler; while the Daleks themselves, well, they seem a composite of various Nazi characteristics. As Terry Nation himself said:

> I did try to include something of the Nazis, that unfeeling, icy-cold mentality. That, no matter what you did, you couldn't deflect them. I've always felt that was the SS in a way. So I like to think that was part of their [the Daleks] motives, part of their characters.[4]

In the first Dalek story this is highlighted in a scene where the Daleks make a form of the Nazi salute with their sucker arm. In their second story, *The Dalek Invasion of Earth*, we visit a London occupied by these cyborg Nazis evoking, so soon after the war, the nightmarish doomsday scenario of German victory. Even as the threat of the Nazis receded into history, there were those that tried to keep their spirit alive. *Remembrance of the Daleks* was broadcast between the 5th and the 26th of October 1988, but it was set in the London of November 1963. This was a time of increasing immigration and growing anxieties about the consequences thereof – anxieties which were thoroughly exploited by right wing political scaremongering. Casual racial prejudice was routinely experienced by many immigrants, and in 1958 riots took place in Notting Hill that involved attacks on British West Indians and their homes by groups of white youths. Accordingly, in this story we see a group of British Neo-Nazis that has allied itself to a faction of renegade Daleks;

---

[4] Terry Nation cited Peel, J. (1995) 'Terry 'Dalek' Nation: A Man of Ideas' Starburst #200

as a statement of where the writer, Ben Aaronovitch's, sympathies lie, in *Doctor Who* terms, this is about as unequivocal as it gets. Should Enoch Powell's direful 1968 prediction of the 'rivers of blood' which would result from immigration have been proved correct, there would, this episode seems to suggest, be only one party to blame: not the immigrant communities, and, no, not the Daleks, but those elements within British society at the time which embodied the Dalek-like characteristics of conceit, prejudice and unalloyed hatred.

The Daleks have, of course, continued to evolve, which must have been something of an inconvenience for a species that as early as *The Daleks* (1963-64)[5] had already defined itself as perfect. Much of this is due to the interference of Davros, who soon realises that he hasn't entirely succeeded in his attempt to create an obedient master race. Constructing a monstrous race only to have it turn on him, Davros is similar to Frankenstein; unlike Frankenstein, however he maintains his interest in his creations, though this does not stop them, like Frankenstein's monster, turning on him. They kill those closest to him first – his colleagues and collaborators in the place of friends or family – despite his pleading, 'No, wait! Those men are scientists. They can help you. Let them live. Have pity!'

Of course the Daleks have no understanding of the word 'pity': Davros had never included that in their makeup. Yet despite his failure, somehow he survives extermination –

---

[5] Or should that be *Genesis of the Daleks* (1975)? That's the trouble with a series based on time travel.

not to mention being left in his bunker for centuries – and as soon as he is able to begins his work once more. His continued attempts to recreate the Daleks to his own specifications lead to the creation of a number of factions, which in turn lead to a number of campaigns of purification by the original Dalek faction. These Dalek civil wars must have been very beneficial for the rest of the universe, since it would have slowed down their expansion across space.

It seems that the Daleks themselves are not immune to the Frankenstein effect. In *Daleks in Manhattan* and *Evolution of the Daleks* they step into Davros' shoes and attempt to refine the Dalek formula. By fusing their DNA with that of humans, they succeed in creating versions of themselves that have the human qualities of imagination and a willingness to question orders. There can be very little more frightening for a Dalek commander than to hear a subordinate say, 'Why?' Nor can there be more anything more thrilling for a youngster constantly being ordered around by adults! I can still remember my joy at the apoplectic rage and frantic, uncomprehending fear with which a Black Dalek reacted, in *The Evil of the Daleks*, to an anonymous Dalek's questioning of his orders.

I suspect I'm not alone in this. A commentator on a documentary I once watched suggested that children identify themselves with Daleks because they share that same sense of frustrated rage with the universe. I could certainly relate to that rebellious Dalek: I felt the same way whenever my parents wouldn't allow me to stay up late and watch TV. I must have dreamed of a Dalek-me taking revenge on the world of grown-ups many times.

It was this ambition that led me to enter a Sugar Puffs 'Win a Dalek Competition' in 1966. This was a promotional event to publicise the new film *Daleks – Invasion Earth: 2150 A.D.* starring Peter Cushing, Bernard Cribbins, Jill Curzon and Roberta Tovey as Dr Who, Tom, Louise and Susan respectively. As in the first *Doctor Who* film adaptation released the year before, *Dr Who and the Daleks*, the Doctor is not a Time Lord, but an eccentric human scientist. He is joined by Special Constable Tom Campbell (who fulfilled the same role that Ian played in the TV series) his niece Louise (a stand in for Barbara) and his granddaughter Susan (effectively a younger version of the Susan of the TV show). But a more explicable deviation from the TV series is the design of the Daleks – a more impressive build than that of their TV cousins. For a start they were filmed in colour and because of that they were made colourful. The drone Daleks were predominantly a metallic and light blue. All the film Daleks looked more solid and streamlined, with thicker skirt bases and an absence the vertical rectangular metal vanes around the mid-section. The two head speech indicator lamps were also larger than the TV versions. In addition to the plunger 'hand,' some Daleks were also equipped with claw like pincers. Instead of the screen going to a negative format when the Daleks fired their guns, as with the early TV versions, the film Dalek guns fired a jet of gas, similar to a CO_2 fire extinguisher. I rationalised this, potentially naff effect by deciding that the Dalek gun's energy beam was ionising atmospheric water molecules into a short-lived superheated steam cloud.

I entered the competition in the hope of winning one of those very same Daleks, no doubt with dreams of trundling down the high street, the envy of my friends, threatening all around me with extermination.

The competition provided a list of attributes necessary for fighting the Daleks; the challenge was to arrange them in order of importance. These were:

(A) Be able to imitate a Dalek voice
(B) Have a protective suit against Dalek ray guns.
(C) Carry emergency food and water pills for a week
(D) Know how to do first aid.
(C) Be able to travel anywhere in space.
(F) Have knowledge of electronics.
(G) Carry a radio to contact Earth from space.
(H) Have resistance to brain-washing.
(I) Know how to operate Tardis[6].
(K) Be as clever as Dr Who[7]
(L) Know how to tell other people what to do.
(M) Never panic in danger

I had a strong interest in military history at the time, so I used my knowledge of military campaigning to make my choices. (C), (G) and (I) went straight to the bottom of the list: these, I reasoned, would only be useful if you planned to escape the planet. Imitating a Dalek... well, I supposed

---
[6] This should have been written capitals thus, TARDIS because it is an acronym.
[7] There was no J because it might have been confused with I on the entry form.

that could be useful, but mostly for frightening other humans. A cool head in a crisis, food and water, plus leadership, electronics and first aid skills seemed to me to be the priorities.

I must have come close because, though I didn't win the main prize – one of three life size Daleks – I did get one of the five hundred runner-up prizes: a Louis Marx battery-operated Dalek (I wish I still had it – they're worth a lot of money now). This was probably for the best: I hadn't thought too much about what my parents would say about a life-size Dalek sharing my bedroom with me!

Just like the Cybermen, the Daleks have had to move with the times, as new generations of writers adapt them to speak to contemporary concerns. The first Dalek story of twenty-first century *Doctor Who* was simply called *Dalek*, but the real villain seemed to me to be the capitalistic despot called Henry van Statten.

Like *Genesis of the Daleks* much of the story takes place in an underground bunker. Like Davros (and Hitler towards the end of the war) Van Statten rules from this underground bastion and wants to exploit the eponymous Dalek to further his own ends. Early on in the story we get to see the power this Van Statten wields as he decides, almost on a whim, that the elected President of the United States of America should be replaced. In the process, again almost on a whim, he fires one of his aides and then effectively orders his destruction by condemning him to a life of homelessness on the streets. Again he orders this in a casual, whimsical self-amusing way: 'Wipe his memory; put him on the road someplace. Memphis, Minneapolis. Somewhere beginning with M…'

The Dalek in this story represents a highly advanced form of alien technology that the capitalistic Van Statten would like to exploit. In fact Van Statten has acquired a great deal of wealth and power by collecting alien artefacts and reverse-engineering them. Of course, this was only done where there was profit in it for him:

> This technology has been falling to Earth for centuries. All it took was the right mind to use it properly. Oh, the advances I've made from alien junk. You have no idea, Doctor. Broadband? Roswell. Just last year my scientists cultivated bacteria from the Russian crater, and do you know what we found? The cure for the common cold. Kept it strictly within the laboratory of course. No need to get people excited. Why sell one cure when I can sell a thousand palliatives?

He further reveals his regard for people after the re-energised Dalek escapes its confinement. As the base's security guards attempt to stop its advance by engaging it in a crossfire they find themselves totally outclassed and outgunned, but Van Statten's concern is for his 'property:'

> VAN STATTEN: Tell them to stop shooting at it.

> GODDARD: But it's killing them!
> VAN STATTEN: They're dispensable. That Dalek is unique. I don't want a scratch on its bodywork, do you hear me? Do you hear me?

Van Statten has no qualms about dissecting the Doctor either, once he discovers that he is also an alien. Others, alien or human, are just there to be exploited by him and he seems to have no checks or balances on his power.

Often it is the 'mad scientist' that is depicted as irresponsible, pursuing activities without any concern for the potential consequences. In this story it is the capitalist Van Statten who believes he can exploit something for profit, but never considers the dangers of attempting to do so until it's too late and the consequences were revealed. Without any checks and balances to curb his excesses Van Statten is confident in his own invincibility that he can't recognise the danger of what he was doing.

We're forced by the story to compare the two; Daleks and Van Statten. The Doctor points us in the right conclusion:

> Do you know what a Dalek is, Van Statten? A Dalek is honest. It does what it was born to do for the survival of its species. That creature in your dungeon is better than you.

But at one point even the Doctor seems to become worse than the captive Dalek as he attempts to exterminate it by electrocution and is unable to resist the desire to torture it to the point where the Dalek asks him to, 'Have pity!' We see a Doctor that has been driven almost insane by the sight of a surviving Dalek after the mass genocide he himself has wrought to rid the universe of them. It is left to Rose to show compassion to the despairing, forlorn, unusually verbose and articulate, cyborg.

Inevitably a design makeover was required for the twenty-first century century *Who* Dalek. Faithful to the original classic design it nevertheless looked more solid and angular and warlike. It was a bronze colouring, which immediately made it seem heavier and more solid. Bronze being the metal colour closest to khaki it also made it look more military.

We see further reflections of our twenty-first century anxieties in *Bad Wolf* and *Parting of the Ways*. The Emperor Dalek it seems somehow survived the Great Time War, presumably by living in isolation for years in the equivalent of a cave in a remote mountain range. Wherever he was he hadn't been idle: his design had been updated (though it remained in keeping with his appearance in *Evil of the Daleks*), and he had busied himself with attempting to rebuild the Dalek race by using human beings as raw materials. The Emperor Dalek has always represented a kind of gold standard of Dalek values. But here he ended up a loon who thinks he has become god, his army of Daleks (who seem equally as batty) are prone to shout things like 'Worship him!' and 'Blasphemy!' in a barbed commentary, in part at least, against religious fundamentalism.

The idea that a Dalek army could be built from genetically modified humans first appeared in *Revelation of the Daleks*. Again we see two factions of Dalek: those created by, and loyal to, Davros, and those loyal to the original supreme Dalek. Davros is intent on replenishing his forces by using cryogenically frozen bodies as raw material. Such a debasement of Dalek purity is abhorrent to the Supreme Dalek, who is so focused on eliminating these deviants that he and his troops act relatively benignly to the humanoids of the story. Why the Daleks loyal to Davros did not share the Supreme Dalek's feelings, I don't know; in fact, Davros' Daleks seemed little better than robots, something like the Minions in *Despicable Me* (2010). And just what fear or anxiety were they supposed to represent? Better dead than Dalek?

In many ways HG Wells' vision of us 'wearing' mechanical bodies has already come true. One of my very earliest memories is of watching a bulldozer and other earth-moving equipment on a construction site. I was fascinated by these machines: how they worked in an organised and coordinated way, pushing great mounds of earth and gravel with ease. It is difficult to describe the impression it made on me; even now, whenever I see a JCB at work it takes me back to that day. For a while afterwards I became obsessed with playing with a toy bulldozer, using it to push sand into miniature mounds. I suppose I was learning to comprehend what I had seen. These were not machines being 'driven' by men, but some sort of gestalt being, a combination of machine and flesh and blood. In other words a cyborg, though obviously I wasn't aware of the terminology back then. And when we 'wear' these mechanical bodies, when we become these cyborgs, I believe our thinking is altered accordingly. We only have to consider the way some people behave when they become a human/car cyborg. They believe that other road users – pedestrians, cyclists, people in cheaper and smaller cars – are somehow inferior to them. Some would like nothing more than to exterminate them, but have to make do with reckless tailgating. Sometimes I'm tempted to think that the Dalek within is beginning to assert itself.

The 'alien' in science fiction gives us an opportunity to speculate on the possible future of our species. The Daleks are the direct descendants of the cyborg Martians from *The War of the Worlds* and the subterranean Morlocks from *The Time Machine*, but the creation of the Daleks by Terry Nation in 1963 was also an expression of the anxieties felt at that time. The Daleks are creatures totally dependent on the technology that literally surrounds them. And as we become increasingly dependent on our own technology, we have become increasingly willing to allow potentially irreparable damage the ecology of our planet in the search and exploitation of fossil fuels. Increasingly, I think, the Daleks represent what happens to a society where the individuals within it rely far too much on their motorcars. They develop the cyborg mentality, equating the sum of themselves and their cars and an intolerance of anything they encounter they deem inferior to their cyborg selves. For decades we have truly believed that we do not need to adapt to the environment, but that we can make the environment adapt to us. We are like the Urban Spaceman of the song: 'I'm the urban spaceman, baby; here comes the twist — I don't exist.'[8]

---

[8] 'I'm the Urban Spaceman' by the Bonzo Dog Doo-Dah Band released in 1968

CONCLUSION

I had always assumed that artificial beings were a thing of pure science fiction, but in fact it seems that they have lived in our collective subconscious for some time, generating myths, legends and fantasies that appear in many cultures and time periods. When we see the technological artificial beings in *Doctor Who* it is easy to forget that they are the latest manifestations of a recurring theme. But *Doctor Who*, with its forays into science fantasy, can bridge that gap between the human artifice of myth and the industrial age. The Weeping Angels take us back to an age of magic and the inexplicable and, like *The Keeper of Traken,* reminds us that statues were once believed to be capable of moving. It is during the Enlightenment, the beginnings of science in conflict with religion, that there is seen an ambition to 'correct' flawed humanity by distilling everything but reason and logic from it. The paradigm of the Enlightenment was that the universe, including man himself, was a form of clockwork mechanics that, once fully understood, could be corrected and improved. *The Girl in the Fireplace* and *Deep Breath* turn this assumption into a kind of parody with the literal concept of human body parts being used as spares for clockwork beings, while Swift's warning of the

Houyhnhnms are echoed in the Cybermen. Good and bad cannot be so easily defined in human beings and the final destination of Enlightenment may not be all that we had wished for. We are still living in a post Enlightenment age and science still strives to cure our ills, but it seems that the more we discover the more we find there is to unravel about how we and the universe actually work.

Frankenstein began his attempts into defeating mortality by researching the occult, but it was only after he was persuaded to abandon these studies and take up science that he achieved his goal of creating a being from the assembled parts of deceased humans. Mary Shelly wrote her book at the beginning of the industrial revolution and it is very likely that it was greatly influenced by the increasing application of science in everyday life. Like the student Frankenstein, science is now approaching the real possibility of creating an artificial being. Both the desire and fear of that potential achievement is expressed in the literature of science, of which Shelly's book was probably the first true example. Throughout there are the themes of mimicking God, although lacking the true power and wisdom to contend with the results, themes that resurface again and again in science fiction. And these themes are not just confined to artificial beings but dangerous and unpredictable technologies. What is created may not remain a servant, but change into something that threatens to destroy us. *Doctor Who* reminds us of this anxiety. The first artificial life we may create could be a sentient computer; we will be creating life within the machine. If we ever succeed we had better be prepared to face up to the consequences of whatever it is we create. We have already become dependent on computers; increasingly we are being conditioned to obeying them, following their instructions without question. Perhaps then it is only a short step for sentient computers like WOTON and BOSS from *The War Machines* and *The Green Death* to start taking control of our minds indirectly or directly. Like Daleks we seem more comfortable when we are obeying orders, but even an order to kill millions with a weapon of mass destruction might prove too much for most individuals. It would seem sensible to take that awesome responsibility away from a human and put our weapons of mass destruction under the control of machines that have no emotion or empathy. They can wage destructive wars, dispassionately and repeatedly killing millions, just as Mentalis did in *The Armageddon Factor,* with the same efficiency as they would any other programmed operation; be that packaging baked beans or operating traffic lights. On the other hand if could instil into them enough compassion, in a way that CAL in *Silence in the Library* and *Forest of the Dead,* and the Interface in *The Girl Who Waited* had, they may be exactly what we need to help us deal with our faults, failings and vulnerability.

I grew up thinking that robots and androids meant machines built of components made of metal, plastic and rubber. But the tradition of robots in science fiction started with biological creations of Mary Shelley's *Frankenstein* and Karel Čapek's *RUR*. Indeed the word 'Robot' comes from the later. One day, maybe sooner than we think, it might be possible to create biological robots. But if they look and function so much like us will we still be able to see those biological robots and androids as machines? It would be likely that their 'manufacturers' might create some obvious distinguishing features of these living androids, like those in Robert Silverberg's *Tower of Glass* that were hairless and whose skin tones were selected from primary colours. This might help their owners see them as machines, but what about them? Won't they decide that the differences between us and them are too insignificant for them to remain slaves? The Gangers in *The Rebel Flesh* and *The Almost People* thought so and so did the Doctor. To paraphrase the old saying, if something walks like a human, talks like a human and feels in the same way as a human then, in essence, it is human. *Doctor Who* also makes the point that beings can be turned into biological robots by a ruthless conqueror, as the Ood and human Robomen were. This illustrates the thin line there is between a 'being' and an 'artifice'. All this begs the question; just what is it exactly that defines us as human?

This of course is one of the main purposes of robots and androids in science fiction. For a long time in human culture it was assumed that it was the belief in a God given soul that separated us from other animals. In a post Darwin world I'm no longer sure if that would suffice to distinguish us from self-aware constructed beings. In the film *Ex Machina* (2015) the question is asked whether there are elements to our make-up that stop the majority of humans becoming psychopaths or sociopaths. Is it enough to create self-awareness and intelligence? Where does empathy and affection come from? Crucially these are stories about the nature of human beings and the definition of life.

There is another function that robots and androids perform. When science fiction presents us with robots, these robots also become a metaphor for science and technology itself, representing humanity's interaction with the technological. They therefore encapsulate our hopes and fears and whether or not we will be able to maintain control. In *The Girl Who Waited* we have seen how our view of the universe is imposed onto the machines we build, imprinting our own limited perspectives in them. If they encounter something unforeseen, would they even comprehend it was different and adjust their behaviour accordingly? Maybe it will be the same with the safeguards we build into nuclear power stations?

I started reading and watching science fiction as a young boy, not because I was fascinated by the metaphors within, but because I enjoyed being entertained by extraordinary stories. I still do, though now I enjoy science fiction at many levels. This element of entertainment is particularly important in stories such as *The Robots of Death*. The writers notably used robots to revitalise a well-known Agatha Christie-esque paradigm by making the murderer an Asimov-style robot. Robots are similarly used to add complexity in Anthony Hope's story of political impersonation, *The Androids of Tara*, as the androids become dopplegangers. There is also that tantalizing prospect of escaping to worlds populated by androids allowing us to live out our wildest fantasies.

Alien robots are yet another facet of the artificial being that have their role to play. One of these is to represent the superior technology of an alien threat whilst distancing their alien masters from us and, if well conceived, they can also emphasise the alien quality of their masters. It may even transpire that what we think of as the alien masters turn out to be biological robots working in conjunction with mechanical robots, as I suggested was the case in *The Dominators*. The most advanced, and strange, alien robots serve ancient aliens that have transcended across universes, so making them seem to us like supernatural beings. These beings in *Doctor Who*, inspired by HP Lovecraft, have automaton that increasingly become more like something from the pages of horror and this has allowed them to fit right into the style of twenty-first century *Doctor Who*. In doing so they smash the concept of a predictable clockwork universe and replace it with strange matter particles and bizarre energy that do not seem to play by the rules we have devised. Ironically the universe has become a stranger place now than it was in Copernicus' time.

There is that twist of fear that human-looking androids add to a story, a recurring theme with anything non-human that looks like us. But when robots and androids disguise themselves to become doubles of specific people it takes our fear that step further. The scenario of android impersonators is the literal representation of our fear of being replaced by machines. They also represent all our fears of the enemy within, the spy and the double agent, undermining the trust and cooperation we have in each other. This was Doctor Who reflecting the Cold War, where opposing ideologies undermined our security from within, just as the replicated humans in *Spearhead from Space* and *The Android Invasion* did. People you think of as friends and colleagues turn out to be deadly enemies, impeding our ability to defend ourselves by working as a team.

It surprises me that whenever the Doctor encountered some independent race of robots or androids that, I never questioned their desire for conquest. They were machines and they were bad. But why would a culture of robots have ambitions to conquer? And how did they end up becoming independent of biological masters anyway? Independent robots are rather like method actors; they have to find their motivation and this may be the original purpose their creators built them for. The Movellans in *Destiny of the Daleks* original purpose might have been to help their masters in wars of conquest. The Roboform in *The Christmas Invasion* and *The Runaway Bride* may have been constructed to scavenge for new technology in addition to being hired-out mercenaries. In *The Mysterious Planet* the final instruction of its former masters is what motivates the alien robot Drathro. In all other respects it is free to do what it wants. Like the Handbots in *The Girl Who Waited*, their view of the universe, imposed by their designers, creates their limited perspectives. After their liberation these artificial beings continue to function within this model of the universe. In all other respects they perform as independent thinking beings, but they are still slaves to their long dead masters. If we are tempted to feel smug or superior to them because of this then we shouldn't. Our world view is likewise a result of the programming that evolution has created. Species of independent artificial beings it seems are no more or less independent than we are.

Despite the increasing use of artificial replacement body parts, the cyborgs we see in *Doctor Who* are still a long way off. What we see in medical science today is, generally speaking, a work-in-progress substitute for our correctly functioning biological original parts. We are forced to resort to them because of disease, or injury, because our bodies haven't evolved to withstand the longer average lifespan we are now living. Of course this need for replacements is driving the march towards creating the cyborgs of science fiction; beings with synthetic parts that are better than the originals. The question we have to ask then is would we still be human if most of our bodies were replaced with synthetic parts? Is it our bodies or our minds that define us, or a combination of both and just how traumatic would that transition be? I am reminded of what one of the characters called Thomas Dodd said in the Big Finish Cyberman story called *Spare Parts*. He is appalled after encountering a freshly converted Cyberman and remarks on one particular feature of the encounter: 'Disgusting. Stank of antiseptic.' This one phrase brought it home to me the impact that such an extreme conversion must have. Minor surgery is bad enough, and there is always that lingering smell of antiseptic associated with it. No wonder the emotions need to be suppressed, a Cyberman would go insane if they weren't.

We know that it was the ambition of the Enlightenment to one day make man perfect and free him from his darker, baser qualities to become something of pure logic and reason. Christianity taught that this would only be possible for the human soul that could move on to a better existence when the corrupt and corruptible body was finally discarded. In creating their perfected being, the science of the Cybermen also had to discard most of that corruptible body, but what remained had no soul. It was no longer human but instead something akin to the walking dead.

The cyborgs in *Doctor Who* seem disconnected from society, half machine people that cannot truly integrate themselves into a community where they are despised, mistrusted and feared. This applies just as much to the Cybermen who are a pariah race of the Whoniverse, but of course they do not have the ability to care anymore.

If we consider the Cybermen a result of the Enlightenments objective of creating the perfect human being, the Daleks can be considered as a kind of antithesis of this. They are humanity with all the good bits taken out. Perhaps it not obvious, but when we are looking at the Daleks we are looking at the very worst that we can be. They were a creation in the mind of Terry Nation that were modelled on the Nazis and HG Wells' Morlocks and Martian cyborgs; themselves extrapolations of human evolution. They can be considered worse than the Cybermen, who at least were the result of good intent even if the results weren't. The Daleks represent the literal evolved or mutated monster that we may become, but in a sense they are the monster we have already become. Like them we have become dependent on our own 'shell' of technology and in order to maintain that shell we seem to be willing to damage the ecology of our planet in the search and exploitation of fossil fuels, minerals and cheap nourishment. Today they are less about the Nazis and more about globalised free market neo-capitalism that is obsessed with accelerating economic growth that cannot be sustained by a finite planet, with a fragile ecosystem. Each of us in our motorcar becomes the Dalek in its metal travel machine, willing to see more and more damage to the environment as long as we can survive as a motorised cyborg content to see the environment adapt to us.

Coming soon from Candy Jar Books

GANGSTERS: A LIFE FOR A LIFE
by Phillip Martin

A novelisation of the classic gritty 1970s British drama. John Kline is an ex-SAS officer recently released from prison who finds himself hired by the secretive DI6 police organisation to go undercover in the Birmingham underworld. Infiltrating a violent gangster organisation, Kline soon finds himself making some dangerous enemies, with his loyalties trapped between two opposing forces.

Gangsters is a novel of money, power and violence, the story of racketeers who grow fat on the profits of illegal immigration, drug trafficking – and death.

ISBN: 978-0-9954821-2-8

Available from Candy Jar Books

LETHBRIDGE-STEWART: MUTUALLY ASSURED DOMINATION
by Nick Walters

The Dominators, the Masters of the Ten Galaxies, have come to Earth, and brought with them their deadly robotic weapons, the Quarks!

It's the summer of '69. Flower power is at its height, and nuclear power is in its infancy. Journalist Harold Chorley is out of work, and Colonel Alistair Lethbridge-Stewart is out of sorts. Dominex Industries are on the up, promising cheap energy for all. But people have started going missing near their plant on Dartmoor. Coincidence, or are sinister forces at work?

Join Lethbridge-Stewart and uneasy ally Harold Chorley as they delve into the secrets behind Dominex, and uncover a plan that could bring about the end of the world.

ISBN: 978-0-9933221-5-0

Also available from Candy Jar Books

LETHBRIDGE-STEWART: MOON BLINK
by Sadie Miller

July 1969, and mankind is on the Moon. Both the United States and Soviet Russia have lunar bases, and both are in trouble.

Back on Earth, Anne Travers has learned she is about to be visited by an old friend from America, Doctor Patricia Richards. Lance Corporal Bill Bishop is aware of the visit, and is on hand to meet Richards.

She brings with her a surprise, one which the Americans and Russians wish to get their hands on. But the only man who can truly help Anne, Colonel Lethbridge-Stewart, is away in Scotland.

It's a game of cat and mouse, as Anne and Bishop seek to protect the life of an innocent baby – one that holds the secrets to life on the Moon.

'Once again, Anne Travers takes the lead in the proceedings while Lethbridge-Stewart is relegated to the background, but for this story that dynamic not only made sense, but is essential. Sadie Miller exhibits a natural knack for writing these characters, and has a strong voice with which to do it.' – Shaun Collins, Travelling the Vortex

ISBN: 978-0-9935192-0-8

Also available from Candy Jar Books

LETHBRIDGE-STEWART: THE SHOWSTOPPERS
by Jonathan Cooper

'Nuzzink in ze vorld can schtop me now!'

There's a new TV show about to hit the airwaves, but Colonel Lethbridge-Stewart won't be tuning in. With the future of the Fifth Operational Corps in doubt he's got enough to worry about, but a plea from an old friend soon finds Lethbridge-Stewart and Anne Travers embroiled in a plot far more fantastical than anything on the small screen.

Can charismatic star Aubrey Mondegreene really be in two places at the same time? What lengths will ailing entertainment mogul Billy Lovac go to in order to reach his audience? And is luckless journalist Harold Chorley really so desperate that he'll buy into a story about Nazi conspiracies from a tramp wearing a tin foil hat?

There's something very rotten at the heart of weekend television, and it isn't all due to shoddy scripts and bad special effects.

ISBN: 978-0-9935192-1-5

Also available from Candy Jar Books

LETHBRIDGE-STEWART: THE GRANDFATHER INFESTATION
by John Peel

The late 1960s and pirate radio is at its height.

Something stirs in the depths of the North Sea, and for Radio Crossbones that means bad news.

Lethbridge-Stewart and his newly assembled Fifth Operational Corps are called in to investigate after the pirate radio station is mysteriously taken off the air, and a nuclear submarine is lost with all hands.

ISBN: 978-0-9935192-3-9

Coming Soon from Candy Jar Books

PATTERN OF DEATH
Peter George

The pattern began in the cold heights of the sky ten miles above the flatlands of East Anglia. A new and revolutionary jet fighter was being tested at supersonic speeds.

Before long the first death slipped into the pattern as agents of a foreign power tried to sabotage the prototype fighter that would give Britain aerial superiority in the Cold War.

Into the mix came Driscoll, called back to work undercover by an anonymous branch of government security, to confront the threat. Little did they know he had already been approached by the other side.

The twisted web of events led through the streets and night clubs of London, out to the windswept military airfields and up into the empty wastelands of the stratosphere.

Through a trail of intrigue and violence the pattern was finally resolved on the concrete floor of the fighter's hangar. But not before many had died and others revealed as something very different from their supposed identities.